A LOVESICK NOVELLA

HEART-SHAPED BOX

L. RENÉE RICHARD

Cover Design by: Designs By Charly
https://www.designsbycharlyy.com/

Interior Formatting by: Designs By Charly
https://www.designsbycharlyy.com/

Editing by: Havoc Archives
https://www.thehavocarchives.com/

CONTENT
WARNING

This story contains explicit sexual content and is intended for readers over eighteen. Other topics may be triggering to sensitive readers.

Please check my website, L. Renée Richard, for more details and a complete list of trigger warnings, further information, or updates if there are any concerns about your mental health. Your well-being is my utmost concern, so please proceed with caution.

BLURB

Mari feels unlucky in love. Expecting a present from her boyfriend, Nate, on her birthday, she gets more than she bargained for. The next day, on Valentine's Day, she receives a package that she hopes conveys the words she so desperately longs to hear.

I need you. I love you. I can't stand to be without you.

Unfortunately, there is only one word that strikes her right through her heart.

Lovesick.

When she thinks her day can't get any worse, she finds out she is wrong.

Swearing off relationships, she tumbles into the arms of Chev, a guy who has always seen her.

One heart-shaped box, some heart-shaped candies, and a dose of karma may be the recipe to revive her lovesick heart.

DEDICATION

Heart-Shaped Box is a novella based on the original short story for the Lovesick Anthology. Since the story had to be within a specific word count range, this is the complete novella that shows what happened before Chev and Mari and the conclusion to the story. I hope you enjoy it.

Lastly, this story, despite the name, isn't a Valentine's Day novella. The novella goes out to everyone who has felt they weren't seen or been alone for a holiday. I think we've all been there. We tend to post happy moments on social media when, more often than not, we are sad, feeling alone, or in our heads. Just realize that you are special, and others probably feel this way. Reach out to your neighbors and friends, perhaps foster a pet, and be the change we all need.

More importantly, you are enough and worthy of happiness. My husband likes to remind me that he loves me 365 days a year, and if I didn't know that yet, he said he needs to up his game. I hope you all find your Mr. Richard out there.

PROLOGUE

MARI

FAREWELL PARTY

The lights strung haphazardly throughout the mesquite branches twinkle intermittently while the music thumps lightly through strategically placed speakers. Looking out at everyone in the backyard, I sway to the music as rhythmic Chicano beats lull me into a nostalgic trance. That is, until I hear a *"grito!"* called out from someone on the makeshift dance floor, causing me to blink and pull me away from my happy trance. The loud, abrupt shout sets off a chain reaction as other voices attempt to outshout one another. I stifle a laugh and continue swaying to the music until flashes in my periphery catch my attention. Someone nearby is taking pictures. I turn my head sideways just to encounter more flashes going off.

A small line forms while friends and family members I have known for most of my life patiently wait to take their picture against my mom's handmade backdrop. I lean my body to take a mental image. To appreciate and later remember the elaborate paper floral wall, boosting vivid colors that showcase our Mexican heritage. It surrounds most of the deck entrance in bright blues, orange, green, purples, and pinks. It's nothing short of stunning, and the image causes an ache in my chest that reminds me of how much work my parents poured into this party. Not money, mind you. We don't have much of that. It was the hard work and care that made this so much more. It meant so much more to me. It also reminds me how much I will miss everyone who cares so much to send us off into the next chapter in our life toward adulthood.

The scene in front of me and the familiar sound of laughter from my guests in the courtyard makes me smile. Despite that, I'm lonely. Everyone seems happy—here to celebrate with me as a send-off into my college years, away from everything and everyone I know. That in of itself is scary because, amongst this familiar crowd, I couldn't feel more invisible. How is it going to be when I don't know anyone? I stand alone, feeling unseen despite having a best friend and loving parents.

"Stop this, Mari," I mumble under my breath, sighing into my shirt sleeve.

I look up and lean forward, peering around and admiring it more now that night is approaching. Voices carry on the humid evening air as loud laughter permeates the small gathering of family and friends. "I sure am going to miss this place," I say, speaking more to myself than the figure approaching me. I regard the other decor on the tables in our yard that consist of repurposed items, like the floral arrangements they placed into empty Corona beer bottles. I choke back the emotions, especially when I can feel her stare before I see her. My eyes begin to mist, blurring the scene before me.

Lilith, my oldest and best friend, walks up to me as I lean over the deck railing, blinking back at the tears that threaten to fall and admiring all my family members and friends who came out to celebrate with us today. She bends over, mimicking my stance. "Me too, Mari." She huffs, resting her head briefly on my shoulder before lifting it.

"Lil, but—"

"But," she interjects, pausing to clear the knot that no doubt lodges in her throat, "I think your aunt needs to be cut off." Attempting to lighten the mood, Lilith hits me on the shoulder to point to where Tía Chonita is refilling her margarita glass from the pitcher.

I run my fingers along my lashes, wiping away the wetness so I can focus on where she is pointing her finger. I snort. "Sure. Go ahead and try." I sniff. "She's feisty."

She is all of four feet eleven inches, leaning over the picnic table and holding a bright pink flashing margarita glass that she uses to keep the pale green liquor, making her easy to identify in the crowd of guests. The nearly empty pitcher hovers over her almost overflowing glass. My negative thoughts melt away as I attempt to suppress a laugh. Somehow, my tía is the only one still using her party favor.

I laugh softly, throwing my hand outward. "My moms outdid themselves with all the decorations for our fiesta, didn't they, Lil?" Just then, my tía takes a large gulp, enabling her to drain the pitcher's remaining contents, making it all fit into her flashing margarita glass.

3

"Sheesh. Look at her. Would it have been better if she had just drunk straight from the pitcher?" Lil chuckles.

"She's living her best life. Nothing wrong with that." Tía Chonita is the fun aunt who always buys you the best presents and gets along with everyone. I've always aspired to be like her instead of being labeled as a "grumpelstiltskin." That's what I was known as just a few months ago by my classmates in high school because they think I am grumpy, but I'm just an introvert, and I chose not to play into their bullshit high school drama if I could help it. If I am going to have fake friends, I prefer fictional ones like the ones in my books.

Lilith cackles, jarring me once again from my wayward thoughts. "Look at her. I just love her." Said tía is now doing the cumbia with her arms flapping like a chicken. And yet, not a drop of alcohol spills from her glass.

"Now, that's talent." I watch, mesmerized.

An unexpected laugh bursts forth as I watch my tía in action. "Lil, I think that ship has sailed." I wave my hand upward as my aunt, still moving her feet, now tries to get the last bits of alcohol to pour out of an almost empty glass. I place my hands around my mouth, attempting to amplify the sound. "The pitcher is gone!"

We continue to stare at her in fascination. A few fireflies can be seen in the distance, causing me to remember another time when I was a child, running barefoot on this lawn with Lil by my side. I can almost hear our childish giggles. Our sundresses flowed as we pranced through the grass with a makeshift crown of white clover entwined in our braids.

Lilith and I used to catch the luminescent insects in our hands once nighttime fell and then release them shortly after, letting them fly away unharmed. We couldn't bear to capture something so beautiful just to keep it a prisoner in a glass mason jar.

"Something that beautiful needs to be free," I frequently sing-songed. Just two girls dancing under the night sky, free to express themselves like fireflies in all their glory without the stifling confines that keep them from shining brightly. A beacon of light in the vast darkness. There are so many great memories, but as I start anew, along with Lil still by my side, I can't help but be apprehensive as we forge a new path into adulthood. Here's to a fresh start. A journey of taking chances. A year of acceptance. An opportunity to radiate positivity.

Lil must sense my deep thoughts. She nudges me. "What are you thinking about, Mari?" A frown pulls at the corners of her mouth.

Who am I kidding? I am the least optimistic person. Instead, I choose to give her honesty. "I'm nervous about the future. I don't want to grow up, Lil," I reply quickly, tilting my chin toward my tía. "But when I do, I want to be just like her."

Lilith sighs dramatically, placing her hand on her heart. "Yeah. Me, too." She throws her arm around me, much like the first day we met in grade school a decade ago. We've been inseparable ever since. I know that she understands my thoughts without needing to actually voice them. Her underlying tone lets me know she understands my fears, hopes, and dreams without saying anything more.

I decide to lighten the mood. "I was just thinking...Grow up? Pfft. Never." I turn around and walk into the house through the back door, and Lil follows me as we both enter the cold, air-conditioned kitchen, seeking a brief reprieve from the humid Texan temperature. My glasses fog, and I take them off and wipe them on my tank top, reminding me why I wear contacts instead. I am placing my glasses back on when I hear a familiar voice that genuinely makes me smile.

"There you ladies are." I turn to greet one of my moms as she enters the house carrying bags of groceries.

"Hey, Mom." I walk toward her as she places the paper bags on the counter. She smiles and motions for us to follow her as she returns to her car. She's grabbing the ice as we approach her. Lil and I go over to retrieve the rest. "Geez, how much did you get?"

She chuckles. "Too much, and some things for you girls when we drop you off tomorrow. You're going to need snacks. Lil, can you get the bag out of the back seat and give it to Heidi for me?"

"Sure thing. Be right back, Mari." Lil runs over to my other mom, who cooks tons of food on the grill to feed my large extended family. They invited the whole family together one last time before we leave. I walk over to Lil as she strides my way. She throws her arm around my shoulder. "I'm sure going to miss this place and all our memories here, Lil." I throw my arm around her in return.

She glances at me slyly. "Don't worry, Mari. I'm sure we will create new memories in college." She waggles her eyebrows.

"Oh, I bet we will. That's the part that makes me nervous the most." I bring my hand to my brow, looking at more people getting up to dance.

She laughs in agreement. "Come on." Lil removes her hand from my shoulder and grabs my hand instead, pulling me toward the makeshift dance floor. "Let's see if we can get your aunt to do the Electric Slide like last time."

CHAPTER
ONE

MARI

I wake up to a coffee grinder blaring from the kitchen. Letting out a low growl, I bring the duvet over my head, trying to stop the assault on my ears at this ungodly hour. As soon as it stops, I sigh, turning over in an attempt to go back to sleep for just a bit longer. But an inviting waft of coffee summons me from my bed like a marionette pulled by its strings. I'm a sucker for a good cup of coffee, and this Costa Rican blend, which my mom bought freshly roasted, is mouthwatering. I lightly pad over to the bathroom as my parents' voices echo from down the hallway. I put on my hoodie, left discarded on the floor, as I look around my bedroom for the millionth time.

When I wake up tomorrow, I will be in a different room—a different place entirely. I look out the window and sit along the cushioned nook, bringing the velour pillow into my lap. This place was once my sanctuary of comfortable solace. It's where I would snuggle under blankets and read while the sun's rays filled my room. I hope I can find the same in college.

Beautiful shades of pink and blue illuminate the sky. I sigh, extending my arms upward and sideways into a big stretch, then I glance over at the packed bags placed against the wall. I put my hands on my hips. "Let's do this. To new adventures." I fist pump the air then grab the outfit lying on my dresser and step into the bathroom to prepare for the next chapter of my life.

CHAPTER
TWO

MARI

"I think that was the last bag, amorcita." Mom comes over to envelop me in a hug. Her chin rests on my head as she sways us back and forth. "I am so going to miss you, mija." I rest my cheek over her heart, taking in the solid beats. *Thump. Thump.* I almost don't want to let go. The safety net of her embrace makes me hesitant to pull away. Tears form in my eyes as I step back from her, quickly wiping them away before they fall.

She lifts my chin, her eyes softening. "Hey. Why the tears? It's a good day. You and Lil are going to have so much fun in college. Well, not *too* much fun." She rolls her eyes. "Don't do anything I wouldn't do?" She waggles an eyebrow in jest, and I can't help but chuckle.

"Okay, Mom. I promise. I'm just going to miss you both so much." I pull her to me, not wanting to ever let go.

"We'll miss you, too." She pulls back to look me in the eyes. "So much, Mari." Mom finally releases me, turns around, and walks back into the house. I follow and see my other mom standing at the doorway, watching us both with a smile.

Mamá looks at her watch and then at the street as if Lilith will magically appear. "You about all packed up?"

"Yep. I'm ready," I say, looking around to ensure I have nothing left to place in the back.

"Is Lil almost here?" my moms ask in unison.

It causes me to laugh because that is a common occurrence. I check my phone and notice that Lil is again fashionably late. From her text this morning, she should have already been here. We promised to move in together whenever we went to college; now, we are roommates.

When we submitted our request to be roommates during the housing application process, we knew there was a possibility that it wouldn't happen. I insisted that we were bound to get separated, but luck was on our side, and we secured housing together. I don't know what to expect once we arrive, but the email stated that they have people who show you where to go once we get there, including a resident advisor who is a resource person and available to the students throughout the building. I am looking up the move-in itinerary as my phone dings with an incoming message from Lil.

"She says she'll be here in five minutes," I shout to my parents, who went to close up the house and grab their things. They have their pocketbooks in tow, locking the front door as Lil drives up. She jumps out of the car like her ass is on fire as her brother, Luis, pops the trunk and rounds the car in quick steps.

She runs over to me, wrapping me in a big hug. "Luis has to get to work, and he says I made him late," Lil whisper-yells to my moms behind me. We separate from our hug.

Her brother rolls his eyes, having heard every word as Lil intended. "No worries, Lil. I already let them know I was dropping you off." He looks at my moms. "Thanks for taking her," Luis states as he puts her stuff into the SUV. He ruffles her short hair in the annoying way you would expect a brother to do as she pulls away from his embrace, annoyed.

"Hey, uncalled for, bro." He chuckles, walking away.

"Call us when you get settled," are his last words as the door shuts. His hand waves out the door as he speeds off.

My moms share a look. "Okay." Mamá clasps her hands together. "Let's hit the road, ladies." And before I know it, we are on our way—college-bound.

CHAPTER
THREE

MARI

MOVE-IN DAY

The large campus hosts over sixty thousand undergrad students and is expected to be busy with move-in day activities. Countless cars move through the town of a little over a hundred thousand residents. Most of its occupants live in rentals throughout the year or in off-campus housing for graduate school, as well as other upper undergraduate lodging options. Considering it is located in a triangle of three major Texas cities, it has a small-town atmosphere with a trendy urban vibe that makes getting around the town manageable without a car. We find the dorm we are assigned to and pull into line, happy to see it progressing quickly.

"Wow, look at that," Lil remarks, pointing at the people who run up to a car, open the doors, and help bring the bags into the dorms. It's run like a well-oiled machine, as resident assistants, students, and other volunteers work efficiently to move incoming students into their dorms. Finally, it is our turn, and Lil and I jump out of the car in succession. Music blares through the speakers, and Nicki Minaj's song, "Super Bass" vibrates through the large entrance speaker.

A guy walks over to me, smiling. "Hi. I'm Nate. What can I bring in for you?"

I stare at him, unblinking. Beads of perspiration dampen his skin. His messy blond hair hangs in waves and I can't help but want to lift my hand, sweeping it away just to better my view of his pretty face. His head tilts and eyes narrow, gleaming with a thousand secrets like a deep blue sea I want to dive right into despite knowing that doing so could be the death of me. A slow trickle of sweat passes over his mouth, hovering over his bottom lip. The tip of his tongue catches it and his lips rake over the same spot, breaking the seductive trance. It feels like it's been hours staring at him when only seconds pass. "Sorry, what was that?" My cheeks blush in embarrassment. I place my hand by my ear to let him know I couldn't hear because of the music. Definitely not because I was staring at how gorgeous he is.

His eyes shift sideways to someone and then back to me. He points to the door and opens it, grabbing a bag from the back seat. "Where are you staying? I'll bring these up."

I nod, showing him my housing papers with my dorm number. "Here?" It comes out as a question.

"Yeah, that's over there." He extends one of my bags toward

the building up ahead. "Follow me." He doesn't allow me a moment's hesitation as he walks toward that building with me, taking two steps to his one, hot on his heels. I look back at Lil, but she isn't at the SUV, and my moms are handing our stuff off to another volunteer. I run a few steps to catch up to Nate. Dang. He has some long ass strides. I'm almost jogging at this pace.

We pass the colossal speaker and walk in. It's cooler in here, and I thank God for the central air conditioning in my dorm. It would be almost criminal not to have it here in Texas, although not all other colleges have that luxury. His long, muscular, tanned legs move up the stairs gracefully, and I hurriedly shuffle my much shorter ones as he leads me to our dorm room. I am practically panting, thinking I should probably work out more by the time he opens the door.

"Here you go," he declares while placing my bags in the middle of the room. "I'll just set these here while you pick which side you want." He stands there, staring at me as I attempt to catch my breath. My little heart is ready to burst from how he looks at me. His slow perusal of my body stops as he fixates on a bead of sweat that drips onto my ample cleavage. He licks his lips before returning my stare. Then he smiles, displaying his perfect, pearly white teeth, not caring that he was just staring at my chest. My gaze darts toward his mouth, and he must notice it because his lips quirk upward. "Well, I never got your name."

I glance at his toned physique and wonder if all the guys here look like him. "I didn't give it to you." It's bold, and I'm liking this new version of myself. Confident Mari.

One of his eyebrows quirks upward, matching his lip. "Okay." He runs a hand through his messy hair, but his gaze remains on mine.

I laugh, not wanting to be a bitch after he helped me to my

dorm, but I can't help but be suspicious of his intentions. I've been burned before, and the memory still stings. He's way too good-looking, and I can't help but wonder if this is his normal behavior or if he actually wants to get to know me. I planned to start anew, so I decide to shoot my shot. This is what I wanted, right? To be seen? "It's Mari. Thank you for helping me get to my dorm." I flash him a genuine smile.

He nods. "You're very welcome, Mari." He turns to leave but then pauses mid-stride before turning back to address me. "Hey." He hooks both thumbs through the front pockets of his jeans as he rocks up on the balls of his feet and then back down onto his heels. "Um, there's a party tomorrow at our suite." He removes one hand to run it through his hair. "It's the Winding River townhome complex, number 2062." He bites his lip, shrugging. "You should come." He looks me up and down before he turns to walk away. "Bring a friend," he says, his voice reaching around him as he steps out of the doorway and disappears down the hall without looking back.

I take the paper with my dorm information and fan myself. "Is it hot in here?"

"A little," Lil says as she walks in, placing her stuff on the bed on the right side of the room. I didn't even realize I said it aloud.

"Hey!" I run over and jump on the bed. "You didn't ask if I wanted that one." I pout playfully.

She snorts. "Please, Mari, like you care." I hop off, and some more students enter our room with the rest of our bags and my parents trailing behind them. The students welcome us to campus and wave goodbye before leaving.

Mamá closes the door behind her and clasps her hands together. "Okay, so let's get you girls unpacked."

Both Lil and I groan.

MY
SWEETHEART

CHAPTER
FOUR

MARI

WELCOME BACK BASH

"Why are we going to this thing again?" Lil asks as we walk up the street to the townhouse.

I shrug noncommittally. It becomes increasingly clear which residence is hosting this party. People congregate outside on the lawn, hanging out, and the door is open, no doubt letting the cool air escape—what a crime. I wonder what their neighbors think about all the noise, but then I remember that most of this area consists of rentals that house other students, and this complex is probably not the exception.

I look at the scantily clad females frolicking about and then remember what I chose to wear tonight, immediately second-guessing my outfit. One girl is wearing a red lace tank top with a black bra underneath and extremely short, tight black leather shorts. I swear if she bends over, her ass cheeks will show. She completes the ensemble with heeled sandals.

"Great," I mutter to myself. I look down at my short, cut-off jeans. Tugging at the pockets hanging by the leg line, I glance down over my shoulder, but nothing shows that I'm aware of. I'm wearing a black tank top with my old Chucks. I prefer comfort over a twisted ankle, and her outfit looks like a trip to urgent care complete with X-rays. I shudder at the thought.

Lil watches me with amusement. She rolls her eyes. "Come on, let's go inside and check it out." Lil grabs my hand and leads me into the party, where the music is much louder. The screen door closes abruptly after me, and I take my first college party in. The couches are moved off to the side, and many are dancing on a makeshift dance floor in the center of the room. People are making out on the couches, and I look away, embarrassed by their unapologetic public displays of affection.

"I need a drink," I blurt out. "Especially if I am going to be around this." I lift my hand at the raucous crowd before us. It's like high school all over again, but up it another level. I was never good at that scene. I always felt different, shy, struggling with social interaction. Uncertainty lingers in my mind as I look around anxiously.

Lil frowns and pulls me in another direction. "Let's go into the kitchen. I bet we can find something to drink that way." Lil points to where a game of beer pong is set up on the table near the kitchen. Cheers are sounding off, and arms go up as someone dunks another ball into the cup. Shouts of "Drink! Drink!" echo through the enclosed space.

I look outside past the kitchen door to see more people around a fire pit, and that's when I notice someone familiar. Nate fills up red plastic cups at the keg and hands out beers. He seems to know everyone, chatting animatedly with each person in line. An attractive girl holding her cup beams at him, and I tug Lil that way. "Come on. I think I see someone I know."

Lil's eyebrows rise before she extends her arm outward. "Lead the way, girl," she says, quickly following at my heels.

I get in line, looking at my place in the queue to see when it will be my turn. I wait there on edge to see if he recognizes me. But before second-guessing myself, I call out, "Hey, Nate." I smile bashfully, wondering if I've made a colossal mistake in assuming I am that memorable.

He looks at me briefly before it registers who I am. Then he snaps his fingers. "Mari." The deep timbre of his voice makes me shiver.

"Yep, that's me." I feel a jab to my side. "Oof." I look over at Lil briefly before returning my focus to Nate. "And this is Lilith, my friend."

Lil extends her hand. "Nice to meet you, Nate." She says his name like it tastes sour on her lips. The puckered face she's making indicates that Lil doesn't like him one bit. Nate's either oblivious or he's just so self-assured that he doesn't care.

He glances her way and smiles. "Hi, Lilith. Nice to meet you," he says before quickly returning his sights on me. "I'm glad you could make it. How was move-in?" I hear a throat clear behind me.

He hands us our cups of warm beer and winks. "I'll catch

up with you in a bit." Nate smiles at the next person in line, dismissing me. He gets another drink for someone else, starting up another conversation, this time initiated by him, and I am beginning to understand why the beer line is so long.

"Who's that?" Lil asks, her tone unimpressed.

"Oh, he's one of the people who helped carry our stuff to the room." I wave my hand around, attempting to downplay the invitation. "He invited me to this party." I glance around in an attempt not to look at Lil, but when she doesn't say anything, I turn toward her. She raises her brow at me. "Okay." My hand goes up to placate an impending negative comment. "Clearly, I wasn't the only one, but at least I got an invite, right?" I swallow as the following words come out harder than I expect, like I am forcing them from my mouth to share my gloom-ridden feelings. "I-I'm just trying to adapt and not be a fun-sucker. Maybe reinvent myself here?" My gaze drops from hers, and I do not want to face the look she is undoubtedly giving me.

"Mari," she says softly. "Look at me." I know what she is going to say, so I shake my head.

"Not tonight, Lil. I just want to have some fun." Lil is my biggest champion. I don't want her to look at me like that anymore. All my past experiences and feelings have shaped me into the person I am now. I don't want to throw everything I am out the window but learn from and change because of it. With a renewed purpose, I look up this time to meet her eyes with a genuine smile.

Lil must see a change in me. She nods, taking my hand in hers, and a playful smile returns mine. "Okay then, let's go have some fun."

MY
SWEETHEART

CHAPTER
FIVE

MARI

L il and I are lost in the music. I'm blissfully unaware of how long I've been dancing or what time it is. Singular strands of my hair stick to my cheek. Beads of sweat trickle down my back, and I focus on its path as it creeps past my bra. I feel someone come up behind me, rubbing up against where the sweat is, causing my shirt to stick to it. Their hands go to my waist and lean in to pull me closer. Our bodies begin swaying to the beat. I look at Lil to gauge her reaction. She frowns but says nothing.

I turn around quickly, feeling the humidity and alcohol muddling my senses. Nate stares intently at me. "Hey, there."

I shoot him a lazy smile, removing the hair stuck on my lip gloss.

"Hey, yourself." He smirks, watching my clumsy motions and staring at the spot where my hair was plastered on my mouth.

Cheers go up as the song changes. "All My Life" by Falling in Reverse ft. Jellyroll blares through the speakers as the crowd sings the lyrics loudly. Nate grabs my arms, throws them around his neck, and then wraps his around my waist. He nuzzles himself against my neck, and it feels good. His breath skims over my skin. His lips hover just over the salty perspiration on my neck as his tongue darts out, boldly lapping up some of the moisture beading on my pulse point. I can't help but melt a little into him. Maybe it's the effects of the alcohol, or perhaps it's the attention he's giving me that I have been craving for so long. Whatever the reason, the effect his mouth has on me causes another pulse to throb, but this time lower on my body.

He begins sucking on my skin, and I pause, feeling it down to my core, making me clench in response. "N-Nate." His name comes out in a breathy moan that is barely audible in the loud, small, crowded space.

Nate touches me like he knows what he is doing. Should I be worried about that? Maybe, but all I want to do now is feel. It's what I've wanted for the longest time instead of just existing as I have been. He touches me like we haven't spoken only a few words to each other.

But when he does, he says things like, "God, I want to devour every inch of your body." And I don't think I can hear that enough.

He makes me feel like I want to have felt for so long. I see the looks from others, and so many girls are vying for his attention, but instead, he is here dancing with me. He smells of Fireball Cinnamon Whiskey and the worst possible decisions. The latter should concern me the most, but now I don't think about anything except the feeling he elicits from my body.

I move in a little closer, feeling him harden as he begins grinding into me. I gasp as he whispers in my ear, "God, you have the most incredible ass," before he sucks on my ear lobe. My knees almost buckle, but then he proceeds to grab onto me. He's bold, confident, and into me, even if just for tonight.

That's when I remember. I haven't been intimate with anyone since last year when I gave my virginity to my disaster of a boyfriend. Despite how horny I am, I'm not going to sleep with him on my first day here. That makes me somber, and I attempt to turn around, fighting the feeling that thrums in me. He's hot, deliciously muscular, and tall. His dark, stormy eyes meet mine and promise to destroy me in the most devious way. I don't want him to see my fear. Can he sense my apprehension? I also want him to like me, not just take me for a night. Dare I say…respect me?

I see Lil dancing with some girl, taking my mind away from the maelstrom of lust radiating off of Nate and me. When I smile at her, she returns the look, but her mouth turns down in a displeased fashion when Nate continues grinding on me on the dance floor, clearly not sensing my turbulent thoughts, but I don't acknowledge Lil's stare. The lustful haze that was covering my eyes lifts enough to allow me to see clearly. I should get off this dance floor and maybe get some water.

Those were my intentions, but the song finishes, and as I turn around to face Nate so that we can leave, the music jumps into "I Had Some Help" by Post Malone ft. Morgan Wallen. People push past us to get onto the small dance floor. It causes my hair to fall into my face. Nate pushes it back for me, and when I look up, I feel someone watching me.

That's when I am hit with the most beautiful man I have ever laid eyes on. While I am physically attracted to Nate, this man does something more. His stare is intoxicating. It's like he recognizes the ruse I am playing with Nate, pretending to be something I am not. His stare, although intense, is kind. Protective. Safe.

Despite feeling aroused by the way Nate touched me moments ago, I know with certainty that just one touch from this man could ruin me. I'd be hooked from the start. Addicted to him like the worst drug. His nostrils flare, and he looks like he wants to pick me up and spank me for misbehaving. I want to run over to him...or maybe away from him. I'm not entirely sure. Not just from the way he watches me but from the way his gaze makes me feel. He looks...upset.

Nate touching me on the dance floor made me feel many things. The pure animalistic lust that has awoken in me from not being intimate is one thing, but the look this stranger gives me is almost my undoing. It's as if... "He sees me," I mumble under my breath.

His eyes crease around the edges as he tilts his head, studying me more closely. *Did he read my lips? Hear my words?* I see his legs move, and I think he's going to stand up from the couch. But what I failed to see at first is a feminine sun-kissed hand that now reaches up to place a protective claim on his leg. His tensed leg muscles go slack as he moves farther back into the couch. *Maybe he was just trying to get more comfortable. Did I imagine the whole thing?* He turns toward the person, and my mouth makes an "O" as her nails grip his black jean-clad leg more tightly.

I follow his gaze, and that's when I notice the girl attached to the hand on his thigh. I gulp down the feelings that threaten to take over me as an overwhelming sense of sadness fills me.

It seems like time stands still, but it's only been a minute. The song changes to "Beautiful Things" by Benson Boone, and I stand there, unable to move as the voluptuous, honey-skinned girl beside him stands up, holding her hand outward to him, inviting him to dance with her. His lip twitches in amusement as he stands up, towering over her, and a silent conversation between them transpires.

I hide my face in Nate's chest, hiding the emotions that are so obvious. Nate is oblivious, speaking with someone over my shoulder. Is it sadness? Or maybe I'm jealous that they can sense each other's thoughts without speaking. They seem to have an ease and familiarity with each other that screams years of knowing one another.

I can't look at him at this point unless I want to punish myself further by continuing to watch as he follows her to the dance floor. But I clearly am a glutton for punishment because I do. And then I watch them dance. I envy her position at his side, especially how well she compliments him, and swallow that bitter pill as I force myself to look away.

Nate pulls me off the dance floor after conversing with someone else, oblivious to my awkward predicament. His hands lock with mine as he pulls me away. But before following him, I make the mistake of looking back. The tall, lean guy with high cheekbones and eyes the color of mocha and cinnamon swirls burn with warmth as he maintains his heated stare on me as I walk away.

He sways with his date to the song, acutely watching me, but his eyes no longer look at just me. No. Instead, his narrowed stare is pinned on our joined hands. A frown pulls on his face, and wrinkles crease the corners of his eyes much like a moment ago, pulling both downward, accentuating his crescent-shaped eyes. The reaction confuses me, but I force myself to look away and forget that despite the extreme intensity of his piercing stare, he's still with someone else, and so am I.

CHAPTER
SIX

MARI

THE NEXT DAY

"Ugh." I roll over on my dorm-issued, twin-sized bed. "Why does my head hurt so bad?" I mumble, causing Lil to stir in her bed across from mine. My tongue sticks to the roof of my mouth, and I am so thirsty I can barely swallow my spit, but I don't want to risk getting out of bed for fear of hurling my poor decision-making remnants onto the concrete dorm floor in a pool of bile. I moan.

"Geez, quit your sniveling already." Lil places her hand

over her face to block out the light threatening to pierce our retinas with its blinding, happy morning rays of sunshine. "Maybe," she croaks, not finishing her sentence before sitting up and drinking some of the water she had the foresight to place on the bedside table that divides our beds. I hear the loud gulps she takes from the plastic bottle, and I enviously peer over at her, only able to contemplate drinking mine for now.

She groans before she continues. "It's because we both drank our weight in alcohol last night." She plops the water bottle back down on the table and slumps back onto her bed. "Obviously." She throws the last word in as an afterthought. She opens one eye to look over at the clock on the bedside table. "Correction." She pauses again as if it pains her to form complete sentences, pulling the sheets back over her head. "A few hours ago."

We lay sprawled across our beds in our sad, hungover state. I moan, still under the covers when I hear Lil move around in her bed. A moment later, something hits me on the head.

"What the fuck, Lil?" I grab the little water bottle and pop the top, drinking my fill as some dribbles down my chin.

"Don't drink it too fast," she chides.

"Yes, Mom." I giggle, forgetting the throbbing in my head and behind my eyes. I groan, rubbing my temple. "It was fun, though, right?"

She just grunts, and I'm not sure if it was in agreement or not, but I know she met someone last night. I think she said her name was Rory.

"Yeah." She chuckles. "It was fun." She turns back around, dismissing me. "Let's sleep some more before we eat some post-hangover greasy food."

"Ugh, what I wouldn't do for a McDonald's hash brown

patty...or like, five. That should do it." I adjust my pillow before falling asleep to Lil's light snores.

CHAPTER
SEVEN

MARI

I trail behind Lil as we walk down the stairs and out of our dorm building. We rose like the living dead and we now walk through the town's populated college student-filled streets. "For the millionth time, Mari, I don't care if you want greasy hash browns. I need a vat of coffee first. Then we can have all the greasy food you want."

My head is still pounding. "Are we close?" I'm whining at this point because I didn't plan on this level of cardio while still hungover. I'm starting to feel dizzy. "I don't know how far I can walk in my deconditioned state," I finally admit after what feels like miles of torture.

Lil looks at me, amused. "You mean hungover state?"

I shrug. "To-may-to, to-mah-to."

Lil juts her chin forward. "Rory told me about this place that has the best coffee, and I'm sure you can find something to eat there that has enough lard to satisfy your needs." She shakes her head and rubs her temples. She probably hurts just as much, but she doesn't complain.

"Fine," I grunt. "I know what a bear you can be if you 'don't have your caffeine.'" I make a show of my air quotes and mimic a childlike expression.

She rolls her eyes. We turn a corner, and she points. "There it is."

I look up to see an eclectic-looking coffee shop. I stop to read the sign. "Hippie Hollow Cafe. Cute." As she holds the door open, I advance in front of Lil, who gestures for me to enter first. "Wow. This," I take another exaggerated whiff, "smells amazing." I look back at Lil as the door closes behind her, her smile wide.

"I told you," she proclaims knowingly as she strides with purpose toward the counter to order. There stands a beautiful middle-aged woman with kind almond-shaped eyes who greets us. I look down at her brown apron with her name embroidered on the top in a gold cursive script. *Llana.*

"Ladies, what can I get you?" I look at the menu and nod, jutting my chin forward at Lil, indicating for her to order first. Lil steps up to the counter, ordering three espresso shots with one pump of vanilla and a splash of oat milk.

I whip my head toward her in disgust. "Three shots." My fingers are held up, showing the number, mimicking my words. She lifts one eyebrow at me as if saying, "Yeah, so what?"

I laugh. "Okay then." I look over the menu, quickly scanning until I see what I want. "I'll take the large iced vanilla matcha latte with cold foam and oat milk, please. Two kolaches..." I trail off. "Oh, is that a potato pancake? I'll take two of those also." Lil snorts, and I feel compelled to clarify. "One is for you." I see Lil roll her eyes as she looks for a table for us.

I click my tongue. "That's twice you have rolled your eyes at me, Lil. Luckily for you, I know that is your love language, and I am well-versed in it."

"Yeah, I love you a lot today, Mari." She walks over to get us a seat, and it's the one spot I would have chosen by the windows, too. There is so much natural light that the greenery thrives. I slide into the velvety cushioned seating and throw my head back, basking in the heat from the sun, which mixes with the cool air in the cafe to create the perfect ambient air. If I were a cat, I would be on my back, belly up, purring.

Lil approaches and sits on one of the chairs across from me. "Are you purring?"

I immediately sit up, wondering if I did, in fact, purr. I blink a few times, and Lil studies me.

She rolls her eyes, already moving on. "Well, what do you think?" Her hand extends outward at the surrounding interior. I take in the natural elements of rawhide, metal, driftwood, and other decor that make it a cozy place.

I nod. "I like it, but let's see how the food is." I quirk one eyebrow upward.

Just then, our names are called, and Lil returns shortly with our beverages. She drinks her caffeinated sludge as I sip my green latte, smacking the light, cold foam coating my lips. A hint of vanilla collides with my taste buds, sending them into a blissful nirvana as I savor the delightful iced concoction. I am so used to the commercial cafe places that serve burnt-tasting coffee or baking matcha, but this is nothing short of heaven with their extensive roasted beans and tea collection.

I hear a groan, and my thoughts are interrupted by half the kolaches gone.

Lil's eyes roll back exaggeratedly. "Orgasmic," she declares.

I grab the last kolache and bite into it. The sausage and jalapeños are the perfect combo. "Nom. Nom. That's good." I smack in agreement.

Lil nods. "So good." We pick up our trash, placing each item in the designated bin for recycling when a familiar guy walks in.

"Hey, Mom. Sorry I'm late." Her eyes glimmer with amusement.

"Late night, Cheveyo?" she asks. He laughs but doesn't comment as he walks to the back.

Lil hits my shoulder, seeing how my trash remains suspended mid-air as I stand there, watching him walk away. "Who's that?"

I almost drop my stuff while I try to recover from my thoughts of him watching me last night and making me feel so many emotions at that party. Making sure not to spill anything while throwing our food, I shrug, downplaying what is probably apparent on my face. My poker face really sucks.

I return to the table to grab my latte. "Don't know," I say as we walk toward the door. Just as Lil opens the door, the stones of the wind chime on the dream catcher make a gentle, clicking sound to announce our departure, and he looks up at the sound to see me as he returns from the back hall, donning an apron. It says, *Chev.*

He looks down at his apron and then back at me. He smiles slyly in recognition of not just trying to decipher his name but of remembering me from last night. Before he can say anything, I bolt out the door. Lil is hot on my heels after me as I turn the corner.

"Geez, Mari," she wheezes, "slow down."

I do, but it's only because I am also out of breath. But it's for other reasons. And the reason is still standing inside that cafe.

CHAPTER
EIGHT

MARI

I'm just leaving my economics class when I see Lilith deep in concentration, staring at the announcement board next to the cafeteria. I approach her, turning to see what has piqued her interest.

"What are you looking for?" I concentrate on the spot she was just fixated on.

She shrugs. "A job, maybe?"

I kick the toe of my shoe against the cement slab. "You want a job?"

I have to work to supplement my tuition, and part of my work is done at Parker Drugstore, the employment my student advisor helped me get. The store is located near the campus, and although it isn't part of the school's traditional work-study program, they hire students year-round to hold part-time jobs with convenient hours. I started last week, and I know they need another person.

"We have a job open at the drugstore for part-time work. Maybe twenty hours. Is that something you can do?" I pause, but don't wait for her to reply. Snapping my fingers, I continue, "We'd be working together, so that's a huge bonus. A selling point, right? Getting to work with your bestie."

Lil looks at me, her smile wide. "Hell yeah. Sign me up."

I throw my head back, fist-pumping the air. "Yes! I'll let them know the next time I go in. You want to go with me and fill out the employment application?"

Lil links her arm through mine. "Definitely." We make our way out of the building, walking across the campus lawn when I suddenly spot Nate talking to a girl under the shade of a tree. She has one leg slightly bent as she twirls her hair with her fingers, laughing at something Nate said. I stiffen, and Lil tries to distract me, but just as she starts to guide me away, Nate sees me. He taps the girl on the arm in farewell and with giant strides, only takes a second to reach me. Lil's arm tightens in mine, but I tap her arm to let go. She drops it just as Nate reaches us.

"Hey, Mari." I look behind him at the girl walking away with her friends, glancing back at me, murmuring something. I don't have to hear her to know what she says to her friends about me.

"Hi." He kisses me on the cheek in greeting. I loosen my body as the worry abates while in his arms, forgetting how he was just talking to another girl. It's just me and my insecurities that threaten to undermine my feelings for Nate. I have to believe he wants to talk to me, and the feeling is mutual.

"Hey, I'll catch up with you later, Mari," Lil states matter-of-factly.

I nod. She waves and walks away toward her next class without another glance in my direction.

Nate rounds on me. "So, you vanished on me that night of the party, and I didn't even get your number." My hand rests at the hip of my feel-good fleece dad joggers. He reaches for that hand as his fingers graze over the sensitive skin exposed between the elastic band and the bottom of my crop top. My grip releases, and he holds my hand in his, tugging me closer toward him. His other hand grips my waist. I look up to meet his eyes and see a smile ghost over his lips. I lick mine because I feel suddenly parched. He tracks the movement as my tongue swipes across before I bite on my bottom lip. "Is that an invitation, Mari?" My eyes widen at his words.

He laughs softly, clearly enjoying toying with me as he steps back. I immediately feel the loss of his body heat. He takes his phone out and waits. I stare at him in confusion. "Your number, babe," he says as if I am dense, rolling his eyes. My face reddens in embarrassment.

"O-oh," I stammer. I take out my phone, swipe the contacts section, hand it over to him, and grab his. He smirks and begins to type in his number. As I am plugging my digits into his phone, a message flashes across the screen with a provocative picture I wish I didn't see. I quickly finish up and hand it back.

He doesn't look at it; he just pockets the phone and grabs my hand. "Are you hungry?" We continue walking and as he leads me through the campus, that picture is all I can think about.

CHAPTER
NINE

MARI

My gut tells me I should ask, but my mind reasons that we are not together. He repeats his question, pulling me away from my thoughts.

"I could eat." I force a smile up at him, and he nods.

"Alright then. Let's grab something." He leads me to his car parked on campus and we take off. We're driving through the downtown area when he glances at me. "So, what do you feel like eating?"

I shrug. "I'm not too picky." He looks over at me again and nods.

"Alright. I think I know where we can go for our first date."

I turn abruptly to look at him, wondering if he is kidding. "What?"

"Nothing," I reply.

"Okay, second date then," he says as he focuses back on the road in front of him.

"I like the sound of that." I watch him smile smugly as he drives. He knows the words he throws my way hit their intended mark. We pull up to a Mexican restaurant with a walk-up window. In the front are cornhole stations and foosball tables, along with picnic tables to sit on, all placed conveniently under a covered patio.

"Do you want to eat outside or inside?" he asks, jutting his chin toward the door. I look inside and see a guy playing an acoustic guitar.

"Inside." Nate takes my hand and leads me through the door. We walk into the crowded place and he takes me up to the counter to order. I look over at the menu and immediately decide on some fried oyster street tacos. My mouth is watering at the thought. I also order a Jarritos mandarin soda. Nate places his order, and we take our seats toward the back of the restaurant for some added privacy. He places our order number on the table and hands me my soda. I take a big swig and lick my lips, savoring the orange sugary liquid. Something about the way the beverage tastes straight from the glass bottle makes the drink so much more robust and flavorful.

Nate smirks at me. "Good?"

I nod. "Yes, delicious." I place the bottle back on the table as the condensation pools around the bottom.

"Hmm." He moves closer to me. "Can I have a taste?" I nod, pushing my drink over to him, but when I look up, he is leaning over, bringing my mouth to his. His kiss is soft, and his tongue moves against my lips in a silent request for access.

I open my mouth in an invitation, which he gladly accepts. His tongue swirls with mine, and I am lost to sensation.

When he pulls away too quickly, I wonder why. Feeling dazed, it isn't until I hear the server ask if we need anything else that I understand. My face heats, and I realize that I didn't even think of where we were, or care, for that matter. I just want more.

"Maybe later," he says with a cocky wink, and then I realize I said it out loud. I turn toward my food, my face heats feeling embarrassed and confused about what has come over me.

We eat in amiable silence while listening to the songs by the live performer. Patting the corners of my mouth, I exhale. "I murdered those tacos." If I could have licked the remaining chipotle aioli residue off the plate and still saved face, I would have because they were that freaking good.

Nate smiles at me. His phone vibrates, but he ignores it. "Did you want anything else?"

I shake my head. "No, I'm stuffed."

"Okay. I'm just going to use the bathroom before we go." He tucks his phone in his pocket and walks toward the back, where the restrooms are. I sit there a few minutes longer than I'd like, waiting for him to return. I look at my watch. How long has he been in the bathroom? I hope he didn't get the shits from the tacos. Lactose intolerant? It's always a possibility.

The guy's voice is impressive and the acoustic guitar is a perfect vibe for the place. I find myself singing along to Led Zeppelin's "Over the Hills and Far Away," until I spot Nate walking out of the bathroom. His phone is in his hand, and he is texting someone. I pretend not to notice. He doesn't take a seat, so I pick up the cue that our date is over. I stand quickly and he grabs my hand, leading me out of the restaurant. He runs over to his side of the car and slides in, unlocks my door, and I open it, fastening my seat belt and getting comfortable for our ride home.

Nate isn't saying anything, so I try to make conversation. "Are you feeling okay?"

He looks over at me, confused. "Yeah, why?" His brows furrow.

Now I feel awkward. "Um. You just took a while in the bathroom and haven't said anything since we got in the car." He nods but doesn't elaborate. Unsure of how to change the subject, I blurt out, "Thanks for dinner. It was fun." I honestly don't know what happened between that shared kiss at the restaurant and now.

He nods again, but this time he responds. "It was. We should do it again."

I let out a breath I didn't realize I was holding. "Are you dropping me off at the dorms?" He spares a glance at me before signaling to take a left.

"Yeah. I have somewhere to be tonight, but I had a great time." He finally pulls into the dimly lit parking lot. He places the car in park, and I unfasten my seatbelt. "Do you have time to come up for a bit?" I ask nervously, biting my lip. He leans in closer.

"Do you want me to come up, Mari?" His words whisper across my mouth, and I stare into his eyes longer than I should before he reaches around and pulls my head toward him. He kisses me brutally, nothing like the gentle kiss he gave me in public.

No. This time he does nothing short of fucking my mouth, and I pull away just about the same moment his hand disappears under the waistband of my joggers. I'm still holding onto his shirt, wanting to stop whatever this is, but also wanting to straddle him in his car simultaneously.

"Why don't we hang out tomorrow? You can come over,

and we can watch a movie or something." He removes his hand from my pants. I let go of his shirt.

"I think I like that idea," I say softly.

He grabs my hand, lacing our fingers together. "Okay, another date."

I nod and open the door to step out. "I'll take that rain check on coming up, though." I blow him a kiss and walk away. I want to look back but refuse to.

When I make it back to our room, Lil is sitting on her bed with a woman sitting next to her. They have her laptop open and watch something that sounds like a cartoon but with curse words.

"Hi." I walk into the room, throwing my bag on the bed. "I'm Lil's bestie, Mari."

The girl stands and holds out her hand to me. "Hi. I've heard so much about you. I'm Rory." I take her hand in greeting. Rory smiles, releasing my hand before she walks over to her belongings.

Lil stands. "Rory, you don't have to leave."

Rory shoves a pile of books into her bag neatly, zipping up her messenger bag. "It's getting late, and I have a class early in the morning anyway." She shrugs.

I look over to Lil and mouth, *"Sorry."*

She shrugs. "I'm going to walk Rory out."

They both leave, closing the door behind them, and I pick up my phone. I text Nate to tell him what time I get out of class tomorrow since he mentioned meeting up. He reads it, but no response comes.

"Left on read. Great," I murmur as I toss my phone on the comforter. I decide to change into my sleepwear. Lil returns and plops herself on her bed, her hands resting behind her head. She glances over at me briefly with a smile on her face.

"She seems nice," I say, offering an intro for her to tell me more about Rory, but all she does is stare at the ceiling, a slight twitch on her lips.

After a few moments, Lil looks over at me. "It's definitely turning out to be a good first year at college."

I nod. "I couldn't agree more, Lil."

CHAPTER
TEN

CHEV

THE FOLLOWING WEEK

I open the door, feeling multiple eyes on me in a nameless sea of faces as I walk toward the professor at the podium, who hunches over a book. I hand him over my slip with my official transfer papers for this class. He takes my note, matches it with his master list, and then marks my name.

"Please take a seat wherever you can find one." He extends his hand to the seat in front of him.

So I walk over to it and plop down, throwing my bag off

my shoulder and onto the floor beside me as I slide into the seat that is way too small for my large stature. Apparently, no one likes to sit this close to the professor, so I need to arrive earlier if I want to sit somewhere in the back of the classroom. I look behind me to every chair filled.

Fifty minutes pass by in a blur, and I take notes as quickly as possible. I'm trying to play catch-up since I am a late transfer into this class, but I've at least seen some of the material before. *I suppose that's a good thing*, I think to myself. I gather my books and place them carefully in my bag, which makes me last in the order of leaving despite my proximity to the door. That's when I notice her—the girl from the party and my mom's coffee shop. She hasn't seen me, but I know she would be staring at me if she did. That's what we seem to do a lot of. Stare at each other. If things were different, I might approach her, but she was with someone the last time I saw her, and I'm seeing someone, too. Somehow, that makes me upset when I know it shouldn't. She's no one to me, so why does it feel wrong to say that to myself?

I continue to take my time until I see her walking closer. Then I step in front of her, causing her to bump into me. She startles, oblivious to my deviant behavior.

"Sorry," she begins, then stops when she sees who she bumped into. As her intense jasmine scent envelops me, I can't help but inhale deeply out of some weird automatic response at being so close to her. My eyes shutter closed. Apparently, I also react unpredictably. Because when she steps back, I quickly open my eyes and grab onto her, halting her movements away from me out of reflex. It's like her loss is too much to bear.

She blinks, and those amber eyes, flecked with green and gold, stare up at me. And as I watch those glossy, full lips, I think she will say something, but she just closes her mouth like a fish out of water, trying to take its final breaths. I'm unsure if I was trying to prevent her from falling or just didn't want her to move away from me.

"Fuck," I mutter, my head tipped back slightly. I'm trying desperately not to imagine what those lips would feel like wrapped around my cock, taking me in to the hilt while she stares up at me with those innocent eyes. Her scent is intoxicating, engulfing my senses, and her arm coats my hand in warmth. She looks as shocked as I feel as she pulls her hand away, but her eyes remain locked on mine. Did she feel it, too? This undeniable connection is something that she isn't immune to either.

"Chev," she says as she pulls away, causing me to ache from the loss of her heady, floral scent. She touches the spot on her arm that I held against mine moments ago, and her eyes close briefly. As she opens them, she seems lost in her thoughts, the realization hitting her.

I clear my throat and nod. "You remembered." Her jaw hardens as if she is mad at herself for allowing this glimpse of her vulnerability. She tries to appear unaffected when people say things about her or her boyfriend doesn't pay her the attention she deserves. He's a player. Everyone can see it, except her.

I'm happy she knows my name, but just as a smile pulls against my lips, she walks away. A blush creeps up her neck. "What's your name?" I call out to her, but she is already gone.

I know I shouldn't care what her name is or who she is, but the moment I saw her that night at the party with that asswipe, Nate, I felt protective of her. Hope and I have been together since high school. My mom knows her parents well. Since we started college, Hope has expressed an interest in having an open relationship. I was shocked when she said that, but I don't think it has much to do with her wanting to date other people. She just doesn't know how to end our relationship after five years. We agreed to talk more about it later, but maybe it's time to end this once and for all. While I love her, I am no longer *in* love with her. There is no chemistry, just comfort and familiarity.

It should've been more evident when I held this woman and looked into her eyes. The jolt of awareness that went through me shot straight to my dick. I haven't felt that way around Hope this past year. Don't get me wrong. She is a beautiful woman, but she isn't very nice. Her personality has become downright nasty to other women who look my way, but she also wants to see other people. She gets drunk at parties, and I'm over playing the role of babysitter. Although I haven't cheated on her physically, being emotionally unavailable is just as bad. As I walk to the cafe, I wonder if maybe it's time to have that talk we've been avoiding since we came to college together.

CHAPTER
ELEVEN

CHEV

Hope and I met some friends for lunch earlier, but now she keeps avoiding my calls. She appeared distant, like something was on her mind. I'm still here for her if she needs me, but we really need to talk.

"Cheveyo," my mom calls out as I toss my bag behind the counter.

I walk over and give her a quick kiss on the cheek. "Hey, Mom."

She pats my cheek, but as she looks at me, concern etches her features. I shake my head, not wanting to discuss it, so she doesn't ask. Instead, she points to the back of the shop. "Can you please refill the coffee machines?"

I nod as I walk to the back, donning an apron on the way and returning with coffee beans for the grinders. I sneak a quick glance at the table that the girl from my class occupied while she was here, but two other students sit there now. I think one of them is her friend.

I don't want to stare, so I let it go. I restock and wipe down tables after the afternoon rush. Our cafe stays open until nine PM, mainly because students use it as a place to study. I usually work until close, so my mom doesn't have to worry about keeping later hours. When it's slow, I take out my books and read, too. It's a win-win.

I've swept the floors and am wiping down the counters as the sun set about an hour ago. The two girls left, and I sweep around the sole person remaining in the cafe before closing up. My phone buzzes with an incoming text from my friend Mason. It's a picture of Hope dancing on a table with a drink in her hand, wearing a short skirt and heeled sandals. "Great," I mutter. "Another night of babysitting, and I have a test tomorrow I need to study for. Just perfect." I blow out a long breath.

My frustration gets the better of me. "Motherfucker," I roar angrily, smacking my hand on the freshly wiped counters. "I am so tired of this." The guy studying throws his books into his bag quickly, startled by my outburst. I'm usually calm and carefree, but I'm not a pushover, and my sense of decency wins out over my schoolwork priorities. I give the patron an apologetic look. "Sorry, man. It's not you. You can stay until we close. No worries."

But he just shakes his head. "You look pissed. I was heading out anyway. Whatever it is...good luck, bro." He makes a quick dash for the door.

The stones of the wind chimes on the dream catcher hit

the door loudly, and I quickly lock the door before anyone else comes in for a last-minute order. Without another thought, I head out in a hurry to see what the hell is happening with Hope.

CHAPTER
TWELVE

CHEV

B y the time I get to the townhouse, the party is in full effect. I text Mason.

Chev:

Hey bro. Here. Where are you at?

It's only ten o'clock, but you'd think it was closer to midnight with how drunk everyone is. I walk in, navigating through everyone while trying to find Mason, or even Hope, who hasn't bothered to reply to my texts. I look at the table where Hope was dancing on top of in the picture Mason took of her, but there is no one there now, and Hope is nowhere to be found.

Chev:

> Hey Hope. I'm here at the
> party. Where are you?

I don't expect an answer at this point. I feel my phone vibrate and look at the incoming text, thinking it's Hope, but it's from Mason.

Mason:

> Mason: I'm by the kitchen. I saw Hope
> disappear upstairs. She hasn't come back down.

I feel the tightness around my heart, but it isn't from betrayal. It is for her safety. If she was dancing on that table, she was drunk, and now she is upstairs where the bedrooms are. She wouldn't normally do something like that, but then again, maybe I don't really know her at all anymore. People change, and Hope's behavior is from someone I no longer know. Mason spots me from the kitchen and starts walking toward me, but I'm on a mission, so I turn and take the stairs two at a time.

I look around at the bedroom doors and quickly open each one before I walk toward the end of the hall, where a line has formed for the bathroom. Someone comments about how long they've been waiting. That makes me halt in my tracks. Unease settles in the pit of my stomach. I walk up to the door and place my ear against it. A masculine voice comes through clearly.

"You like being on your knees for me, don't you, baby?" I straighten when I hear a woman moan. My hackles rise, knowing that something just isn't right. All the breath rushes out of me. "I'm going to come. Swallow it down, baby. That's

70

it."

Something snaps in me, and I can't take it. Against my better judgment, I open the door. Hope sits on her knees with mascara smeared down her cheeks and red lipstick smeared down her chin. I step back and recognize the guy zipping up his pants before walking past me and quickly dismissing her. I stare at the woman I've been with for five years, now a stranger on the cold, tiled floor before me. She starts to sob when she sees me, wiping at her mouth after she just swallowed Nate's cum like I attempt to swallow down my emotions.

"Are you okay?" I ask her because, first and foremost, I care about her, even if she doesn't appear to reciprocate those feelings. She nods, and that's all I need to know before I walk out the door, leaving her in her current disheveled state.

"Chev!" she screams. "Wait, Chev!" She follows me as I sprint down the stairs. I have nothing more to say to her. I round the corner and see Nate with his arm now around the same girl I haven't been able to get out of my mind. She looks worried. She bites her lip, and I stare between them. Nostrils flaring, I want to bring her into my arms and away from that cheating scumbag, but I've had enough.

"Nate?" She looks at him and then at me. "Is everything okay?"

The cheating asshole takes a swig of his beer. "Yeah, Mari. Everything is fine." But he isn't looking at her. He's looking at me. Daring me to say something, and so I do. It's just not what he expected.

"Mari." I roll her name around on my tongue for the first time. Maybe Nate was expecting me to call him out, but Mason approaches me, running interference before I can say another word.

"Bro, let's get out of here." He leads me out of the kitchen before I do something I'll regret.

MY
SWEETHEART

CHAPTER
THIRTEEN

MARI

He says my name like a plea. Nate's grip on my hand tightens, but it doesn't elicit the same response as Chev. I should take this as a hint, a sign, but he has a girlfriend, and they seem close. I look back at Nate, seeing the stone-cold look in his eyes aimed at Chev.

Is he jealous? Someone approaches him, tapping him on the shoulder. Chev turns and strolls out of the living room with his friend. That's when I see a girl crying at the top of the stairs, calling out to Chev as he leaves, not sparing her the attention that he had once solely focused on her months ago when I first saw them together.

Did they break up? I'm still staring at her until she looks my way, and if looks could kill, then I would be six feet under. She briefly looks at Nate before returning her glare to me. I flinch.

"What did I do?" I ask. I look at Nate, who doesn't spare her another glance.

"Don't worry about it, babe," he replies, pulling me into a kiss.

I pull away, directing my attention back to Chev's distraught girlfriend. One of her friends approaches her, holding her shoes in her hand, and grabs her elbow, leading her away from the stairs and out the door in the same direction Chev left moments ago. I get a strange feeling that I'm missing something, but I sense Nate watching me. When I feel a tug at my hand, I turn toward him. My brows furrow as I search his expression for something, but his face is unreadable.

"What was that about?"

He shrugs. "Fuck if I know." He takes a pull of his beer. "Drama." I don't really believe him, but I don't say anything. I bottle up the intuition that screams there is more to this, and against my better judgment, I let it go.

MARRY
ME

CHEV

TOGE
FOR

CALL

CHAPTER
FOURTEEN

CHEV

MONTHS LATER

Hope and I haven't spoken since that night. I made sure she was okay after I left her, but that was all I could do. She made her choice, and I made mine. While I don't forgive her, I wish her no ill will. I just can't forget how I found her in the bathroom. She tried several times to apologize, claiming she made a mistake, leaving message after message that I ignored before eventually blocking her completely.

We're over, and I've already moved on.

What I can't seem to move on from is Mari. Despite the scene between Hope and Nate, Mari is none the wiser. She continues to be in a relationship with him, and while I hear rumors of their intermittent breaks from one another, I mind my business, continuing with my classes and working in my mom's cafe. I've gone on a few dates, but I'm not looking for anything more than that.

I might reconsider my position on the matter if a certain woman decided to give me a chance.

Like an apparition, she enters the cafe. The light shines through her sheer top, illuminating her luscious curves and making my cock twitch in my pants. She always comes here to study, and when I catch her looking my way, I pretend not to notice. We play this game of cat and mouse. She always sits in the same spot with that same iced matcha latte.

In class, it's the same thing. I sit close enough to her that I catch a faint whiff of her scent and can't help myself as I steal glances her way. She's unaware of my torture. The internal struggle to not claim her. I want her to see me like I see her. To only have eyes for me. Whenever I watch her slide sideways across the path of desks to maneuver into her seat, I can only think about sinking to my knees and burying my face between her thick thighs. My notebook spreads across my crotch to hide the permanent tent of my pants on most days.

She's usually drawing swirls on the outer edge of her notes or other forms of doodling. I watch her as she listens to the lecture, biting the tip of her pencil or her bottom lip when she concentrates or is confused about something. I see everything she does. She is always out with Lil and Rory. They seem inseparable.

I notice everything about her.

Mari shows up to study before I usually arrive at work

and takes breaks from studying to read from her Kindle. I'm pulled from my thoughts when I hear her gasp, and then her face reddens as her eyes track the words, oblivious to how my smile matches hers. She doesn't smile often, but when she does, it's glorious. I want to be on the receiving end of those smiles someday.

My mom comes in, and I'm thankful for the reprieve. My cock has never been this hard. I've been pretending not to stare at her for too long. I need to leave and quit this infatuation with Mari. I need a cure.

"Sorry I'm a few minutes late. I know you had plans tonight." My mother comes over to me, gives me a quick hug, and then grabs my apron from me and places it over her head. I'm just praying she doesn't notice my hard-on.

I glance over at the table where Mari sits, now joined by Lil, and Lil's girlfriend, Rory. She pretends not to have heard our conversation, and I smile. Another part of me wonders whether or not she is curious about what I have planned. After hearing she broke up with Nate again, I almost wanted to ask her out, but I need to be sure.

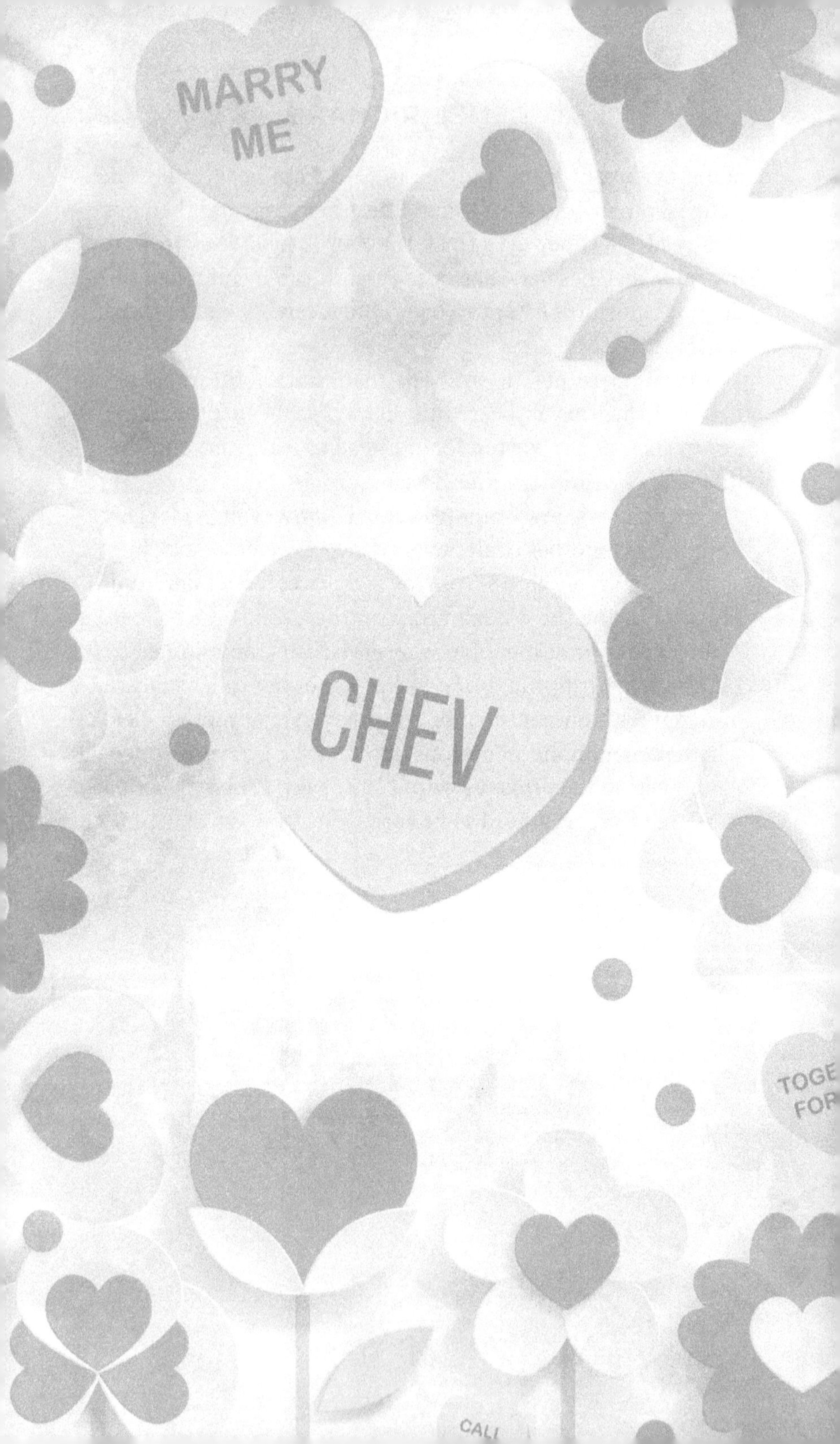
MARRY ME
CHEV

CHAPTER
FIFTEEN

CHEV

I forgot to grab some ibuprofen at the store the other day, so I find myself inside Parker's Drugstore. I look through the aisles and find the medication I need for my horrible headache. Picking a bottle off the shelf, I approach the cashier and see Lil at the register. I place my medication on the counter, and she rings me up.

"Hey, Chev," she says in greeting. "I haven't seen your mom lately. Is she okay?" Lil looks concerned. No doubt my mom has befriended Lil and Mari, as they frequent the cafe most days.

"Yeah, she's just taking a staycation." I laugh. "I think she's finally getting the 'work-life balance' motto I've been hoping to brainwash her with."

Lil's shoulders relax. "Oh, good. I was hoping it was just something like that." I see her expression change to one of annoyance as she hands me my receipt. "Bye. See you later," she says in a clipped tone that doesn't match the conversation we were just having, but then I notice she isn't looking at me. I turn to see Nate place a package of condoms on the counter as I walk away. I'm almost out the door when I hear her say, "It's Lil, jackass. Mari's friend."

How does he not remember her best friend's name? "Jackass, indeed," I huff once I'm outside.

I really need to let this go.

MY
SWEETHEART

CHAPTER SIXTEEN

MARI

ONE YEAR LATER

I stare up at the ceiling, unsatisfied and now fully awake. Against my better judgment, I got back together with Nate after a brief hiatus. Nate pulls out of me and removes the condom, dropping it into a trash can by the bed with finality, like my hopes for just one orgasm tonight. He lies there uncovered on the bed as I cling to the sheets, clutching them to my breasts, wondering how I ended up back here with him. Not just in his bed, but in this toxic situation. Has he always been a selfish lover, or am I just inexperienced?

He pats my stomach with his hand, returning me from my wayward thoughts, not bothering to look at me. "I got a class early, babe," he yawns, "so I'm going to call it a night." I sit up. *Am I supposed to leave?* "You need me to walk you out, or are you good?"

I throw off the sheets and gather up my clothing and remaining self-respect from the floor, getting dressed as quickly as possible. "I'll, um, see myself out." I grab my tote bag and walk to the door. Before leaving, I pause, already knowing the answer to this question but needing to have my fears confirmed. "Are we still on for tomorrow?"

Nate promised to take me on another date since we haven't gone anywhere in a while. We're meeting up at his place after classes, ultimately just hooking up. Well, I'm just getting him off or going down on him before he has another prior commitment. He's been swamped studying and getting tutored for his English class. I can understand the need to maintain a good grade point average, but I feel in my gut that that isn't it at all. I came to this university with plans and goals for myself, but sometimes the best-laid plans don't work out. What I need to work out is why I'm letting myself be treated this way.

He flips onto his stomach, turning from me so I can't see his face. "Sorry, babe." He rearranges his pillow, getting more comfortable and making me more uncomfortable as I wait, not wanting to hear more of his weak excuses. "I forgot I have to do something tomorrow, and then I'll be heading to my parents for the weekend, but we can do that date thing soon, m'kay?" He yawns. "Careful getting home."

He may as well have slammed a door in my face with the way that I feel used and discarded. If he goes to his parents this weekend, I know that when he returns, he won't take me anywhere. Maybe that's for the best. I need to remind myself what a healthy relationship is like, and I know just where to find that.

CHAPTER
SEVENTEEN

MARI

L il and I left campus for the holidays. I needed the break to self-reflect. Seeing my moms and being home surrounded by my family was nice. I explained the situation to my parents about Nate and realized I have to show that I am worth it and won't allow him to treat me that way anymore.

When I met Nate, he was so sweet and took me out. He's always been flirtatious when speaking to other women, but I just chalked it up to his friendliness. He was hiding behind those smiles, lying about who he is—a narcissist. When I expressed my feelings to him, he said I was insecure, making me believe it was true. A part of me *is* insecure, and I know that continuing to go out with Nate is bad for me.

I just didn't want to believe it. I'm not the only woman to fall for this. Sometimes, the face they show differs from the mask they hide behind. Lil and Rory saw it. Lil was never a fan of his, but I didn't want to accept it. I couldn't see it. Holding on to only a few good memories is wishful thinking, too. I was always hopeful that there would be more good times.

"I can't believe he broke up with me and then tried to talk to me today." I groan as I feel my phone vibrate in my bag. Lil and Rory walk with me across campus. I resist the urge to check who is calling. The text messages I left on read should have given Nate a clue that I am never getting back together with him. The holidays are over, so I'm sure Nate has decided we can now resume our relationship.

I am onto him. I am walking his dog and reading his mail. I get it. This is his MO. This is what he does. He breaks up with me during the holidays to avoid the "awkward feeling of having to get each other a gift" phase, as he calls it. We leave for the holidays, making a clean break, which I assume makes him feel better about cheating on me. Then he tries to act like he misses me. My birthday is coming up, and it's also Valentine's Day soon. I doubt he will keep trying for much longer since he'd have to get me a present.

"Fuck my life."

CHAPTER EIGHTEEN

MARI

I turn the blow dryer off, fluffing my hair out. A knock on the door startles me out of my mundane morning routine. "I'll be right there!" I run down the stairs, loving all this space in our new place. I look out the side window to see who is at the door, just as it sounds again. I notice the van idling in the driveway.

"Foster's Florals. Hm," I mutter to myself, reading the vehicle logo. "Just a sec." I unlock and open the door with a massive smile spreading across my face. I can't help it. After all, he remembered.

"Hi. I have a delivery for a..." he trails off, glancing at the invoice. "Are you Mari?" I nod, transfixed on his hands. He is holding a black heart-shaped box, and I gaze at the present longingly.

"Yes, I'm Mari." I practically beam at him. My smile spreads by the second. "Is that package for me?" I can't hide my enthusiasm pouring from each spoken word. I bounce up to my toes, waiting for him to hand it over, rocking on my heels like a kid anticipating their Christmas gift from under the tree or, in this instance, my birthday.

"It is," he confirms. "I just need a signature here." He hands me the touch screen, and I scribble an illegible signature on his keypad with the stylus. He places the box into my eager hands and walks off. I turn around, kick the door closed with my foot, and set the gift on the table, eyeing it greedily.

"Eek!" I screech, jumping up and down. "I can't believe he remembered my birthday after all." I grab the sides of the box and open it carefully, not wanting to ruin the beautiful box. I pull the cover off. I am hit immediately with an aromatic, floral smell. Inside are two dozen red roses. "Oh, wow." I have never seen something as beautiful as this. It's stunning. I stare in wonder at the simplicity of the arrangement, yet the bouquet and presentation are opulent. "Whoa, he went all out on this one." That's when I notice a card sticking out of the side. I pick it up. Maybe today is the day I get to read the words I've longed to hear for some time now.

I need you. I love you. I can't stand to be without you.

Well, not that extreme, but anything remotely exhibiting some affection would complete my day. Nate isn't the best boyfriend, but he has moments when I think he cares. I open the card, and my heart stops.

I know it hasn't been long enough, but I can't stand to be away from you. It may be too soon, but I'm falling in love with you, Maxi.
XX Nate.

The card falls from my grasp, seesawing through the air until it reaches its resting spot on the floor. I sense my breathing pick up, and my lips may be tingling. I can't tell for sure. My hand involuntarily reaches upward as my vision swirls in front of me. I instinctively grab the chair to steady myself as colors fade into black-and-white splashes. My vision flickers like the emotions of my rapidly splintering heart. It *has* to be a mistake.

"Who is Maxi?" I voice aloud, cupping my mouth as if the mere presence of her name makes me want to expel the contents of my liquid breakfast. I thought he may have cheated on me, but I never had proof. The times I questioned him, he denied it and I felt ridiculous for bringing it up. He is so charming. Any other times I heard he had gone out with someone, we were on a "Nate-imposed break." I pull the hair out of my face, flustered by the ordeal tying it back with an elastic holder. "There is only one way to solve this. I need to confront him and get answers. I am tired of feeling this way." I continue ranting to myself as I toe on my Chucks and grab my house keys.

I regain my composure, grabbing a big drink of water before shutting the door behind me, and drive to Nate's townhome that he currently shares with three other roommates. I don't waste time. I'm a girl on a mission to discover what is going on. I grab the box, close the car door, and run up a few steps, knocking on the door before I have time to think twice about my impulsive decision.

When I think no one will answer, the door swings open, and I see a tall girl with bright blue eyes and her hair piled on her head in a messy bun. I stare at her, wondering if she's one of his roommate's girlfriends. Unease settles in my stomach as we exchange stares. She tilts her head to the side, studying me.

I clear my throat. "Is Nate here?" I hold on to the box, and her line of sight turns to it. The thin line of her lips dissipates, replaced with a smile that forms on her face.

She looks at me expectantly. "Is that the mix-up with the flowers?"

"Excuse me?" I stare at her, and her smile widens.

"The flowers," she repeats, pointing at the heart-shaped box I'm clutching as if my life depends on it. I blink, not understanding what she's saying. "Are you here to correct this..." She looks down and turns around as if looking for something. "Just a second." She disappears, leaving me standing there. She returns a minute later, holding a small floral arrangement of carnations, lilies, a few roses, and a mixture of daisies. "Thanks so much for coming over to correct it."

She grabs the box out of my hands before I can protest. "Nate was upset they gave me someone else's order, but the names were similar, so it's unsurprising. Here, you can take this back."

She places the little vase adorned with a pink bow in my hands. I want to tell her something—anything—but no words escape me. "Oh, and here." She reaches into her pocket and thrusts a ten dollar bill at me, shoving it into my hand that holds the little vase. "For your trouble. I know you guys also work on tips during this busy holiday delivery time." I stare at her stunned, unable to speak. "Bye." She turns abruptly, closing the door. I stare at the bouquet, card, and ten dollars in my hand. I place the flowers on the step and decide against the better judgment to open the card. I take a deep breath, bracing for the blow I know is about to come and hit me straight in the heart. Let's be honest. I don't have the best judgment. Otherwise, I wouldn't be in this situation with a guy that everyone but me can see is unworthy of my time.

I bring the note up to read it, mouthing the words.

> Happy birthday, Mavi.
> I hope you have a great
> day.

It doesn't say anything else. There are no terms of endearment or declarations of love. Not even his name personalizing the arrangement. What the hell was the point then? I drop the card beside the flowers onto the porch, leaving only with my cash and a broken heart.

CHAPTER
NINETEEN

MARI

The betrayal I feel is one thing, but the countless rejections I've allowed myself to suffer compound my pain. I decide to leave it all there—the pathetic excuse of a floral arrangement and all the negativity at my ex-boyfriend Nate's house. I can't believe I let him in *again*. New Year's was a blur. He had the perfect opening.

Trying to psych myself out of the downward spiral of emotions, I stare at the ten dollars in my hand. I will, however, take this money Goldilocks gave me and buy myself a beverage at Hippie Hollow Cafe to make myself feel better. "A tip, she said." I snort. "Here's a tip: don't waste your time on such a pathetic, narcissistic prick." I just wished I had followed my own advice and saved myself this feeling.

I have another hour before I have to be at my class, so I take my cash and head over to get my favorite drink—an iced matcha latte. Luckily for me, the line isn't long.

"Hi, Mari. Do you want the usual order?"

I attempt a smile that doesn't reach my eyes and nod. "That would be great, Llana."

She looks me over. "You okay, kiddo?" Concern is etched on her face as I avert my gaze to remove my ten dollar bill from my pant pocket.

"Yes, I'm just peachy." I attempt a better smile, and Llana nods. She adds a couple of pumps of vanilla syrup to my large iced matcha latte and shakes it out, cold foam on top.

"Here. On the house. Happy birthday, Mari."

As she greets the next customer, she wiggles her fingers in the air in a silent goodbye. When she turns around, I drop the money into the tip jar, ridding myself of the painful memory. I take a sip of the liquid heaven and sigh in contentment as I walk to campus.

I take my time and enjoy the scenery before me. The park in the center of town is beautiful. I feel like a haze has lifted and even though the hurt was real, I have a sense of clarity. The air is cool and I think about how I would love to sit under one of the trees and read my book sometime, but I don't have time today. I have a class to get to, and then I have a shift at Parker's. I can feel the tension and disappointment of today dissipate with each step I take toward school. Just because my day started terribly doesn't mean it will worsen. I put a little pep in my step as I focus on happy thoughts: kittens, blue skies, and iced matcha lattes.

I am still mentally echoing my positive affirmations as I walk into the school, heading for my next class, until I hit a wall of muscle, which causes me to bounce backward.

I take that back.

This *is* the worst day of my life.

I'm now drowning in matcha as I stand there looking around, wondering what the actual fuck just happened. My mouth is still hanging open, and I look down at my now-drenched shirt and wasted beverage all over the floor. I'm holding onto my cup, crushing the plastic so hard that it squeezes out the remainder. I drop the cup because, at this point, what difference does it make? What's another few ice cubes hitting the floor?

"Oh my fucking God." I blink and then see him. He's looking at me like he isn't sure whether to run, help me clean up, or hold me as I break down in tears.

"Let me..." He reaches a hand out to me. "Mari." I blink a few times, clearing the tears that begin to form a veil across my vision. As his hand touches my arm, I feel a shiver rack my body, and I shudder at his touch on my wet arm.

I walk off. I think I hear Chev calling after me, but I honestly can't be sure. The sound of my heart beating loudly in my ears causes everything else to be muffled. I take long strides, and as I turn the corner, sure that I am out of sight, I stop to catch my breath. I look down at my outfit and shake my head in disgust. Regaining my composure, I pull my shoulders back and walk toward the bathrooms. I place my book bag on the counter and dry myself, wiping the green evidence away. I gather soap from the dispenser and attempt a quick bath at the sink because that's exactly what I need. Luckily, my hair and face remained unharmed, so just a quick change of clothes, and I should be good as new. My pride took the worst hit.

I ruffle through my bag and pull out my work uniform. I planned on changing into this after class, but I have no choice without another set of dry clothes. It's just some khaki pants and a polo-style shirt with the drugstore logo, but it's not an outfit I would ever wear to class. Most kids in my class don't have to work while in school, but I was not born into such a life. I have work-study a few days a week in the library this year, and after school, I still work part-time as a sales associate at Parker's. Having both incomes allows me to purchase some additional luxury items like expensive caffeinated beverages.

I fasten the second button of the shirt, straighten it, and turn around to check out the back. I sigh into the mirror— no more procrastinating. I have to get to class. I walk past where I spilled my drink moments ago, but the mess has been cleaned, and a wet floor safety sign marks the death of my matcha.

I walk in while my professor is mid-sentence, feeling the entire class stare at me. Heat rises to my face, but I find my seat and quickly drop into it. I close my eyes and shudder. I can feel Chev eyeing me, but I can't return his stare. I've wanted his attention, but not like this. I am mortified.

Yep, worst day ever.

CHAPTER
TWENTY

CHEV

"Cheveyo? Are you going to daydream, or will you replenish the compostable to-go cups?" My mom's dainty, brown hand rests on her hip. Her body language radiates annoyance, but her almond-shaped eyes are kind and alight with humor. She looks behind her, uses her Jedi mind tricks to read my thoughts, and glances toward the empty spot where Mari usually sits. "Hm." Mom brings her finger up to rest briefly on her chin. "Let me think about this. You weren't by chance fantasizing about a cute little Latinx girl who usually takes up residence in that particular corner of the cafe, now would you?"

"Mom." I raise my hand. "Stop. I am not talking about my love life with you." I shrug, quickly making myself busy refilling the cups. She wasn't too upset hearing that Hope and I had broken up. Now I'm more available to help my mom run our family's cafe when she needs me to, and I don't complain about some of the perks associated with this job, like staring at Mari. We've pretended not to notice one another for countless months. I'm more enamored now than I've ever been. It's not like I'm stalking her, but if the gods are trying to set us up, then who am I to disagree with divine intervention?

"So, you *do* admit that there *is* a love life with Mari." I just walk past her, dismissing the intrusive questioning as I pull an apron over my head. The wind chimes ring on the entrance door, and a peaceful sound rings as Lil and Rory walk in. "Hey, Lil. Hi, Rory. What can I get you?" I look behind them and then at the door, wondering if maybe Mari snuck in with them or if she'll magically appear. Lilith's stone-gray eyes shine brightly with amusement. She looks at Rory, and they somehow have a silent conversation amongst themselves as I squirm under their scrutiny. Lil returns her attention to me, amusement now gone. "I'll take a plain latte with oat milk." She turns to her girlfriend. "Babe, what do you want?" Rory pretends to look at the menu, and Lil's bewitched gaze firmly fixes on her.

I scoff, and the spell breaks as Lilith looks at me, her thin, angular eyebrows turning inward before her verbal lashing will surely ensue. I raise my hand to Lil. "Save it," I say, laughing. "I meant no disrespect. It's just that Rory always orders an iced dirty chai with oat milk. Let's see, what does she say? Oh, yes. 'It's the perfect blend of espresso and tea.'" I look at Rory, who stifles a laugh.

"Well, he isn't wrong, Lil. I guess I need to change it up a bit, huh, Chev?"

I look at them, shaking my head. "Nah, Rory. You do you. I was just messing with you."

Lilith shakes her head, now laughing as I ring her up for the drinks. I step away from the counter, deciding whether to ask about Mari. Against my better judgment, I hand Rory her drink first, and then as I give Lil her drink, I blurt it out.

"Hey, how's Mari?" I hate the way I say it, all rushed and breathy. I curse under my breath. Rory spits her chai over the counter, sputtering in laughter as I look around and proceed to wipe up her mess. Eyebrows raised, Lilith seems wary.

"Why do you ask?" She stands straighter, ready to defend her friend. "Because if it's about that ex of hers, the birthday ruiner—" She stops when I look at her quizzically. Her face snaps to Rory, who is shaking her head.

"What ex? Nate?" His name makes me gnash my teeth together in anger. "Wait, what did you say? Today is her birthday?" I look at both of them, but they remain tight-lipped. My mom walks past me, obviously eavesdropping on our conversation.

"Of course it's her birthday." She pats me on the shoulder. "Even I know that. I gave her an iced matcha on the house. She looked like she could use a pick-me-up." She waves. "Hi, Lil. Hi, Rory."

"Hi, Llana." Both girls wave back at my mother, smiling brightly. She ducks out of the conversation, wiping a spot of spit and iced chai I missed, leaves us, and walks toward the back storage area.

"Ugh. I bumped into Mari and spilled that latte all over her. She looked so sad, and I..." I stop before the words escape me, but they do not go unnoticed. Rory elbows Lil.

"You know," Rory pipes up. "Don't you guys work tonight, Lil? At the drugstore?" Lil catches on to Rory's schemes, nodding vigorously.

"Yep, sure do. Maybe you could bring Mari another iced matcha and cheer her up?" She shrugs. "Or don't. Just an idea." They both leave with Cheshire cat smiles spreading across their faces before I can ask another question.

My mom comes out coincidentally at the right time as the wind chimes above the door sound, announcing their departure. "So..." she starts, dragging out the word. I don't want to have this conversation, but knowing my mom, she'll keep asking. I turn toward her.

"Spit it out." I roll my hand in front of me, visually pulling the words out of her. "I know you can't wait to tell me."

She bites her lip. "I think you should do it."

I cross my arms defensively across my chest. "Do what?"

"Bring her a drink at work." She shakes her hand above her head in an *I can't believe you can be this dense* motion.

I nod. "I'll think about it."

She shakes her head, throwing her hand in the air as she walks away. "Sometimes men are so dense," she mutters under her breath as she walks away. I don't have to think about it, though.

It's about time I got the girl.

MY
SWEETHEART

CHAPTER
TWENTY-ONE

MARI

The Valentine's Day candy shelf is almost empty, it being the day before the most loathsome commercialized holiday ever. I grab the restock merchandise and open one of the cardboard boxes with my box cutter. As I gaze down at the contents, I groan in aggravation as a metric shit-ton of heart-shaped boxes stare down at me. I throw my box cutter down, and it stabs into one of the boxes. "Take that, you stupid box of candy." I bend over to retrieve my work tool as Lilith watches me, trying to conceal her laughter.

"Girl, what did that poor candy ever do to you? You're

getting all hostile on the wrong object." I sigh, knowing which object I should be taking out my hostility on, but it's futile. I begin to reshelve the items for last-minute shoppers who either forgot about the holiday or decided to get their significant or not-so-significant other a last-minute gift.

Lil angles toward me to help put the candy away. I'm happy she's working here tonight. Otherwise, I would be alone with my thoughts about how I seem to be unlovable. Sensing my emotions, Lil grabs my arm, causing me to look at her. "Want to talk about it? I suspect it has something to do with your deadbeat boyfriend?"

"Ex-boyfriend," I clarify. I nod, though, nonverbally confirming her questions. "We are never, ever getting back together."

"Okay, Taylor...but fuck, Mari. Why do you put up with that piece of shit loser?" I shrug, trying not to laugh at her Swiftie comment and being unable to speak for fear of crying. I am not a hugger, and neither is Lil, but I can sense her need to hug me at this moment. She doesn't push me to tell her, but something about Lil makes me want to confess my transgressions like a sinner at a church altar.

"You know, the worst thing about this doesn't even have to do with Nate." I pause, looking up at Lilith. "It's that I ran into Chev at school." I place my hands over my eyes, shaking my head in shame. I don't continue.

"Wha—" She raises one hand over her head for emphasis. "How is that the worst thing after all you've told me today?"

I groan, reluctantly thinking about that embarrassing moment when I was drenched in my beverage. "Well..." I clear my throat. "Llana gave me an iced matcha as a birthday treat. I was so in my head about today's events that I ran straight into him on my way to a class we shared. My matcha spilled everywhere, dousing me in green tea." I groan. "I was so embarrassed, I fled the scene and had to change into my work uniform. It's all I had but I'm lucky that I did."

A smile plays at Lil's mouth as she tries to suppress her laughter.

"I was late to class and couldn't even look at him when I had to walk in mid-lecture."

Lilith's wide smile threatens to break out into a full-blown belly laugh at my expense. She takes in the story's events while popping heart-shaped candy into her mouth. I stare at it disapprovingly. All I see are heart-shaped items mocking me, reminding me I don't have anyone to give my heart to.

"Here," Lil says, motioning for me to put my hand out. I take the offensive candy into my palm, noticing the words on the little multicolored treats. My lips tighten into a thin line. I raise my head, and my gaze catches on Lil, who stares at me curiously.

"This has got to be the worst-tasting candy ever. It's like candy corn or, better yet, the Tootsie Roll candies handed out to trick-or-treaters. You know, the Halloween candy that no one wants."

"Puh-lease, spare me the dramatics, Mari, and just eat the damn candy. I have to run back to the storage room." Her keys jingle as she walks away and leaves me there, holding the candied hearts in my hand.

I pick one up. *Kiss me.* Another one. *You're sweet.* I scoff and pick up a third piece of chalk-tasting candy. *I love you.* I pick up the first one again and throw it in the empty cardboard box. "How about..." I think for a bit, touching my chin with my index finger. "Fuck me." I toss it to the side before picking up the next one. "So *not* sweet." I throw it with a flick of the wrist. I hold the last offensive candied heart with particular distaste. "Like I'll ever hear the words 'I love you.' Nope. Fuck you, too." As I throw it into the trash with the rest of the little hearts, I feel someone staring at me. Expecting to see Lilith, I stagger back as I meet Chev's fervent, chocolate-brown eyes.

I don't like how he's looking at me. The way he sees me—sad, vulnerable, and unlovable. I didn't expect anyone to hear me talking, least of all the boy I have the biggest crush on. That is the entire reason I frequent *that* coffee shop. Maybe not at first, but he's definitely the reason for my continued visits. I sometimes find myself staring at him and forcing myself to look away when he glimpses my way, probably feeling it when I watch him, but I've never expected him to reciprocate those feelings. My own biological mother left me when I was young, but I try never to allow myself to think about that. Because someone did choose me, and my adopted mothers are the best. They make me feel special and have always told me they love me, but some part of me wants to be special to someone—to be loved romantically.

Instead of saying anything to him, I turn around and run from the situation. I faintly hear my name being called as I round the corner and go to the storage room. I see Lil's keys in the lock, and I enter, turning on the light, but she isn't there. I hear a door close, and once again, it isn't Lilith. Chev examines me.

"Why are you here? It's for employees only." I wait for an answer, but he doesn't say anything. "You know what? You've never talked to me, so why start now?" I shake my head, walk past him, and my arm brushes against his. I feel the hair on the back of my neck rise, which sends a chill down my arms and makes my fingers tingle. I reach out for the door and turn the handle, but it doesn't open. I try again, and nothing.

CHAPTER
TWENTY-TWO

CHEV

"Mari." It slides easily off my tongue. I remember the first time I said her name. It was under different circumstances. When she was still with Nate.

My words fill the small space, making it feel stifling in here. I see her jiggle the door handle, but to no avail. We're locked in. I repeat her name, this time with more conviction. "Mari, look at me." Her fingers still but remain wrapped around the door handle. I saunter toward her, and I can see her stiffen as I approach. I stand directly behind her, bringing my body close without fully pressing against hers. I reach out my hand and cover hers, prying it away from the door handle.

The jolt of electricity I feel that shoots up my arm is unmistakable. I feel her tremble as I run my hands up her arms. I turn her around slowly, and she doesn't fight me. She becomes pliable in my embrace, and instead of backing away from her, I face her. Her amber eyes seize my breath when she looks up at me. Her lips part slightly, and it makes my cock stiffen. I suddenly imagine what it would be like to have those plush, full lips wrap around my cock. It's the effect of being this close to her.

She licks her bottom lip, and I fight back a groan as my cock weeps in anticipation. Our eyes lock. I run my right hand up her arm, glide it along her collarbone, and lightly up her neck. She closes her eyes, but I want her to open them and give me her full attention. I don't want her to hide from me ever again. She is all I see. I want her to know that. I need her to know that. My fingers trail up her chin and caress her bottom lip, pulling it outward slightly. When she opens her eyes, we are locked in a tantalizing stare that makes me want to take her against the wall of this storage room, and my knees almost buckle at the thought.

I lean into her, placing my forehead against hers. Mari's breaths quicken. I need to be closer to her. Does she even realize what she does to me? How long have I been staring at her from a distance? My lips skim against hers, and I try to hold back the desire I have pumping through my entire body. It's when she says my name in a whispered moan that my control snaps, and I slam my lips against hers.

I expect her to pull away, but instead, she grabs the back of my neck, threading her fingers in my hair to draw me closer to her. We are starved for each other and I can't get enough. I pull my body flush with hers, and she gasps when I push the rigid bulge in my jeans against her soft stomach. I plunge my tongue into her mouth as she gasps, and I fuck her mouth the way I wish I was fucking her pussy, with an animalistic desire to make her mine. My dick leaks when she grabs my hand and places it on her tit. I squeeze, my fingers finding her nipples and pulling at the peaked buds that protrude through her polo shirt. She picks her leg up, trying to gain more friction from my body thrusting against hers. I welcome the feeling of her hand roaming my body.

"Oh God, Chev," she moans as I suck on her neck, her lower half grinding against my cock. I place my palm against her core, and the heat radiating off of her pussy engulfs my hand. I bite lightly on her nipple through her shirt and the skimpy excuse of a bra she has underneath. She rubs herself unabashedly against my palm, seeking enough friction to get off.

"Mari…" I say her name in between bites and the soft kisses I place up and down her neck. "Come for me, baby." She grinds harder as I smack her ass and grab ahold of it, pushing her up and down on my erection as my other hand rubs her pussy through her pants.

"Oh God, Chev, I'm coming." She begins to scream as I swallow her cries with a searing, all-consuming kiss.

Before she can come down from the high, and I almost come in my pants from watching her orgasm, there is a knock on the door.

"Mari, are you in there?" I hear keys rattle against the lock, and she pulls away from me, eyes wide with pink painted on her cheeks. She looks at me and then at the erection that is poking through my jeans, twitching like it wants to break free of its own accord and finish what we started. A smile tugs my lips as she looks down at her shirt, which has two wet spots from where I bit and sucked on those pretty pert nipples moments ago. Her flush deepens as she pats her hair down. The door opens, and Lilith peeks in, smiling as she assesses us.

"Hm. I'll just leave this door open for you guys. I would hate for you to be trapped in here again. I wonder how that happened." She brings her hands up to her cheek, much like the kid from the movie *Home Alone.* She chuckles and saunters away like the cat that caught the canary. Just as I think Mari is about to bolt, I grab her hand and turn her around. Giving her another quick kiss, I open her fingers and press my lips against her open palm. Replacing my kiss with one last piece of candy, I walk away without looking back.

CHAPTER
TWENTY-THREE

MARI

I stand there, feeling so many things. One of them is relaxation. It was probably the orgasm that made my mind, for the first time in a long time, feel worry-free and subdued. All the negative thoughts—the anxiety and depression I have renting space in my head are fleeting. One moment with Chev serves these thoughts an eviction notice. I just hope he doesn't ignore me tomorrow when I see him in class. Self-doubt begins to creep through my mind again until I remember I have something in my hand. I open it to see it's one of the terrible-tasting little hearts I was mocking when he first saw me.

"Yuck." I glance down at the offending candy. I lick my lips, still tasting the mint from his gum, and my heart flutters, coming alive from its shriveled prison cell. I turn the heart over and read the words.

"Be mine." I say the words out loud, wondering if he means it. It can't be true, can it? Does he want me to be his? Why would he have given this to me if he didn't? Otherwise, he would have just walked off after having his way with me. He didn't benefit like I did. He left with a very stiff cock that he would be resigned to take care of on his own. Oh, how I wish I could help him out of that little, or should I say *big* problem. I only had the feel of him against me, but his cock felt huge. Heat begins to burn at my core, and I miss the feeling of him near me, touching me, just like he did moments ago.

I walk into the employee bathroom and notice the flush of my cheeks. I am still high on my dissipating orgasm. Attempting to fix my hair and adjust my shirt, I frown when I see the lingering wet spots on my breasts. I shiver at the memory. I blast the hand dryer on my shirt and giggle about having to do something like this.

"There." I turn back to see the spots have now dried and then groan. I move my shirt along the neckline. "What the fuck, Chev?" Red spots mark my skin. "Great." Running my hands through my hair one last time, I walk out of the bathroom, bracing myself for what Lilith has to say.

I don't have to wait long. I can see her finish stocking the candies, already placing the marked discount sign in anticipation of the Valentine's Day candy sale, while the Easter Bunny sits idly waiting for its debut appearance. She glances up at me with a broad smile encompassing her face. I can't help but smile back at her.

"Just say it already, Lil." I roll my eyes. She shakes her head, raising her hand defensively.

"Nothing. I've got nothing. But…" She hesitates. "I have to say that I am glad you guys somehow got locked in that storage room to work out the sexual tension that was radiating off you two every time you tried to pretend you weren't into each other."

I look at her, shocked. "What do you mean?" I ask innocently.

"Please, girly pop. Everyone knows but you two. That has been brewing for a while now, and I am glad it finally happened."

I glance over to the shelf and see an iced matcha latte sitting pretty while a slow drip of condensation pools around the bottom of the cup. "Why is that matcha going to waste, Lil?" I look at her, and her smile widens.

"Well, Chev bought that for you since you spilled your drink today. He wanted me to tell you happy birthday."

Shocked, I look at the drink and then at her. "What? Why would he do that?"

Her expression softens. "Maybe he likes you, and you finally have someone who deserves to be in your company, Mari, because you are worth it, my friend." She hugs me, and wetness threatens to spill from my eyes.

I tighten my grip on her before pulling away. "Thank you, Lil, for being my best friend, but…if you ever, I mean *ever*, lock me in a storage room again…" I trail off as she cackles loudly.

"I plead the Fifth, bestie." She raises her right hand as if she is swearing an oath.

I savor the deliciousness of the earthy beverage while Lil resumes eating her nasty little candies. "Hey, Lil?" She turns to me, eyebrows rising as she munches on the little chalky treats.

"Yeah, babe?"

I smile innocently at her. "Do you think I can have the rest of those candies?" She doesn't hesitate and hands them over to me, enjoying the positive energy that radiates from me.

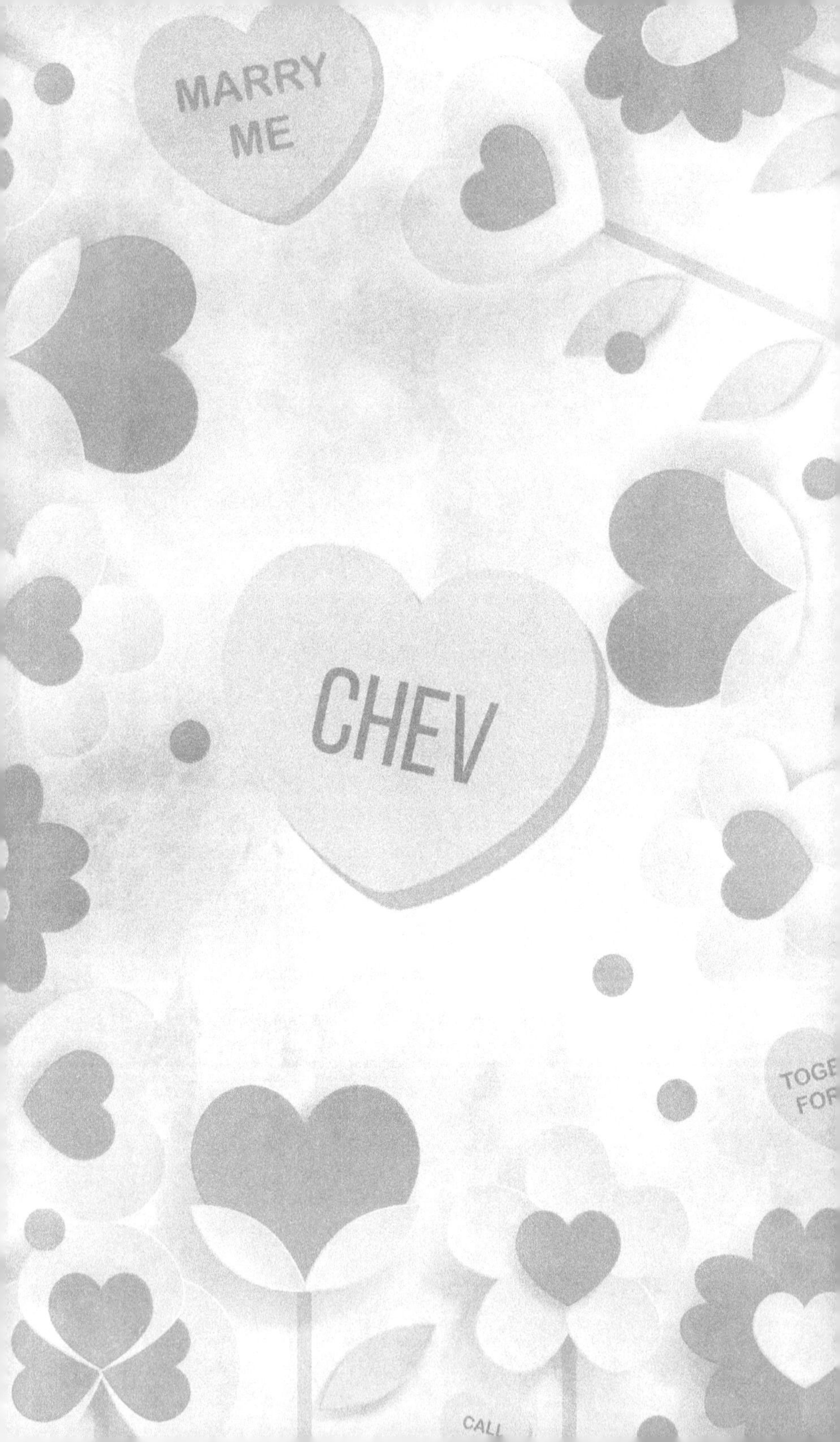
MARRY ME
CHEV
CALL

CHAPTER
TWENTY-FOUR

CHEV

I walk into class with both excitement and apprehension about seeing Mari today. I look around, but I don't see her. Immediately, my thoughts darken as I wonder if I pushed her too far, or worse, perhaps she didn't reciprocate the feelings I laid out for her yesterday. Did I freak her out when I left the candy in her hand? I run my hands through my hair, tugging at the ends in frustration. Just then, I look up to see Mari walking through the door right at the last minute. I exhale in relief as she glides into my row. We make eye contact, but I don't see any expression on her face that lets me know where I stand with her. She breezes by me, and sits at the end of the aisle. I continue to stare at her, but she doesn't look my way.

Disappointment etches on my features, and I try to hide the overwhelming sadness that envelops me. I shake my head, look down at my paper, and notice a little heart-shaped candy resting there.

"I'm yours," I read out loud in a hushed tone. A smile spreads across my face, and this time, when I turn to look at Mari, she is smiling at me. I stand, grab my stuff, and sit beside her. She clearly didn't expect me to move from my seat or to make a public display of affection as I clasp her hand with mine to intertwine our fingers. I face forward as the professor starts the lecture. I can feel her smiling, too.

CHAPTER
TWENTY-FIVE

CHEV

Walking hand in hand back to her dorm after we exchange numbers, we talk and laugh about anything and everything. We took so long to finally get to this point and my cheeks hurt from the crazy-ass smile plastered onto my face. The time with her is over too soon, and I find that I don't want it to end. "Would you like to go out to dinner with me tonight?" Mari looks at me, eyes widening in surprise.

"What?" she questions, but I know she heard me. I chuckle. "Don't you want to have dinner with me tonight?" I rephrase the question as I pick up her hand and bring it to my lips, peppering it with light kisses. She stares at my lips as they hover over her knuckles.

"Hm," she says lazily. "I mean, yes." She nods. "I would love to go to dinner with you." She graces me with one of her radiating smiles. I've longed for it and now, I finally have the pleasure of being on the receiving end of it. I lean in to press my lips against hers. Placing my arm around her waist, I tug her closer and deepen the kiss. She whimpers, and I fight the urge to continue this on her front steps—in view of other students coming and going through the dorms. She looks up at me with big doe eyes that melt my heart.

"Did you want to come upstairs?" she asks sheepishly. Her vulnerability shows as she moves her hands together in a nervous motion. I wipe at her bottom lip, which has smeared lipstick underneath it. She swipes her tongue to lick her lip and, in the process, wets my fingers. I shudder at the feel of it. Fighting the urge to follow her inside her place, I move away from her. Her smile fades, and I hate that.

"I can't," I tell her. She tilts her head to the side, studying me. I never want to make her feel like I don't want her, so I need to explain. "If I do, sweetheart, we will miss our reservations, and I want to take you out for Valentine's Day." Her eyebrows crinkle together in confusion.

"Reservations?" she asks.

"I booked them hoping you gave me the right answer, and if you didn't, I wasn't opposed to begging." Her eyes brighten with humor. As I start to walk away, I turn my head back to see her still staring at me. *That's my good girl.* "I'll pick you up at seven," I shout when I'm almost to the end of the block, and I see her nod in acknowledgement.

My phone rings when I get to my dorm. "Ugh, who actually calls?" I pull it from my pocket and see *Mom* displayed on the screen. "Oh shit!" Worriedly, I pick it up on the fifth ring before it goes to voicemail. "Hey, Mom. What's up? Everything okay?" She gets straight to the point.

"Chev, is there any way you could come and help me out at the cafe? We had a callout, and I'm up to my neck in orders."

"Now?" I groan, rubbing my hand up and down my face. I hear the desperation in her voice.

"Oh, come on, Cheveyo. I really need you."

Knowing I'd never tell that woman no, I acquiesce. "Okay, but I have to leave as soon as possible."

"Yep, fine, just come right now." Before I can answer, she hangs up.

"Damn." I throw my phone down and look at the time. I shower quickly and pack a bag to change at the cafe when my shift ends.

I drive a few minutes to the shop and park quickly, seeing the line of customers through the window. I quickly text Mari.

Chev:

Can you meet me at the cafe instead? My mom coerced me into helping her tonight.

I am pleased to see that she responds quickly.

Mari:

Sure. See you at 6:30.

I walk into the cafe, still looking at Mari's text, when my mother calls out to me, waving her hand for me to hurry up. I quickly put my phone away and get to work.

CHAPTER
TWENTY-SIX

MARI

I decide to take an Uber over to the cafe. I spent time shaving and moisturizing every part of my body so that my skin is silky smooth. I have stared at this guy for over a year, not acting on my feelings because I was dating someone else. I now know that my feelings were not mutual, and Nate does not know the meaning of the term "exclusive."

As if summoning the devil himself, I open the door, and the wind chimes sound my arrival. I come face to face with Nate. There he is, the fornicating fool, sitting at my favorite table in the cafe. I'm frowning more at the loss of my favorite spot than because of my ex-boyfriend. It's crazy how a little treatment from the right guy can put everything into perspective.

Nate stares up at me as I pass by. A fleeting look of surprise in his expression is soon replaced with his usual smugness—his toxic masculinity. He bites the cap of his pen between his teeth in an attempt to look intelligent, but I know that he is barely passing his classes due to laziness more than anything else. The guy puts minimal effort into anything he does, and that will be his downfall in all his endeavors. He struggles to show any type of affection. He left me feeling unheard, unsupported—and, most of all—unloved. I thought I was unlovable from the way he treated me—from the way that I allowed him to treat me.

Nonetheless, he is no longer my concern, so why would I care about that? I just hope another girl doesn't fall into his trap. If I'm ever given the opportunity, I will save the next girlfriend from Nate's emotional abuse.

Instead of my usual table, I take another less appealing one. I'll sit there as long as it is as far away from Nate as possible. I peek toward the counter and don't see Chev. Maybe he is out back. I strain my head to skim around the view of the counter, but nothing. I glance at my watch and see that there's still ten minutes until six-thirty. Looking up, I clutch my chest in shock when Nate stands at my table, his hands in his pockets, peering down at me. "Dear God," I mutter, pushing back from the table.

I gape at him hovering over my table. Annoyance radiates off me in waves. I am not a violent person, but I have never wanted to punch someone in the face as much as I do at this moment, with Nate staring smugly at me. His smirk widens, seeing that he got his desired reaction.

"No need to call me God, darling." He looks me over, and I want to rip his eyeballs from their sockets—the audacity of this guy. I can't believe I thought he was endearing. "Mari," he purrs, "what are you doing here? And dressed up at that?" I look at him quizzically. I don't understand what he's talking about. I always come here, and he knows that, but I don't understand why he cares now. He never cared about anything that had to do with me.

"Did you dress up for me? Were you hoping to get my attention because," he licks his lips as he leans into me like he's about to tell me a secret, "you did, Mari. I'm right here."

My mouth hangs open at his arrogance. Just when I am about to reply, Chev walks up and extends his hand to help me rise from my seat. He gives me a chaste kiss, and I feel his smile as his lips press against mine. Nate stares at our entwined fingers. A sour expression taints his face, seeing us together. I could say something mean or use this scenario to belittle Nate. I could very well make him feel how he made me feel on so many occasions, but I don't. I won't give him any more pieces of me. He will not get my emotions because he no longer ceases to hold me down—to make me feel anything. I'm finally purging all my negative energy and feel a freeing sense of calm wash over me. He doesn't have any power over me, and now that I realize this, I am truly free.

Chev addresses Nate, distracting me from my swirl of emotions. "Thanks, man, for keeping my girlfriend company while I got ready, but we have dinner reservations. Don't want to be late, do we, baby?" I shake my head, holding his stare. His crescent-shaped eyes rise in question and sparkle mischievously. He pulls me to him as we leave the cafe. I don't have to look back to know that Nate is left there slack-jawed, wondering what the hell just happened.

CHAPTER
TWENTY-SEVEN

CHEV

I stand from my seat and pull out the chair for Mari. She smiles up at me as she stands. I grab her coat and help her into it, pulling the sides together as I kiss her forehead. Holding hands, we leave an almost empty restaurant. The service was packed tonight, as to be expected. The conversation was easy, and Mari and I had hours to get to know each other—her more than me.

Things don't feel awkward between us until I'm standing at her doorstep. I don't want this night to end, but I also don't want to make her feel obligated to let me in. "I had a really good time tonight, Chev. It was an almost perfect night." She pulls at the edges of my jacket, and I move the short distance to be nearer to her.

I wrap my arms around the small of her back. "Almost? Well, Mari, what could I do to make it perfect?" I rock her back and forth as her cute little nose scrunches in thought.

"Well, I think that you should come in, and we can figure it out." I search her eyes to see if there is any uncertainty in her expression, but it's not. I lean in and kiss her quickly, pulling back. I turn her around and march her to the door, smacking her on the ass.

"Lead the way, baby." She giggles as she fumbles with the keys to open the door. "Here. Allow me." I take the keys from her and open the door without another moment wasted.

I regard her as she walks around the small space she shares with her roommate. She puts her purse down, goes to the refrigerator, and pulls out two bottled waters. I gladly accept one. "Do you want something else to drink? We have some wine."

I shake my head. "I'll only have some if you are."

She shrugs. "No, I didn't plan on it."

I walk closer to her. "I want to have you very sober to do all the things I want to do to you." She bites on her bottom lip, seeming to contemplate my offer. "I want you to remember it all, Mari."

This time, she extends her hand out to me. "Let's go." She leads me up the stairs to her room. She grabs our waters and places it on her nightstand.

"Where is your roommate tonight?"

Her shoulders lift. "Lilith is staying at her girlfriend's place."

She sits on the edge of the bed, and I watch her begin to unzip her open-toe boots. I kneel at her feet, and she stops abruptly. "Here," I say, grabbing onto her foot and helping her out of her boot. I take the second one and repeat the process of removing her other shoe. I remove my own and approach her as she leans back. I place one knee on the bed as she scoots upward, and I follow, trailing my other leg upward and crawling over to her.

I nudge her legs open with my knees and settle over her. My face is inches over hers as I hold her gaze, fixed on the shimmer of her amber irises. "You're so beautiful, Mari." I lean in, burying my nose in her hair as I skate up her neck, inhaling her jasmine scent. I trace my lips against hers, barely making contact until she reaches up and tugs my bottom lip with her teeth, biting down. I lick my lip, and it tastes like copper. Blood beads over the area where she bit me. Whatever restraint I had cracks, and I lean into her, taking her in for an all-consuming kiss.

I break away, sitting with my cock straining under my pants. Mari's lips are swollen from my bruising kisses and her legs are pinned beneath me. I lift her dress, her thin lace panties wet with her arousal. I groan at the thought of tasting her. I push her dress up and lift her back off the bed, helping to discard her outfit and throw it onto the floor.

She reaches for my pants, and I let her unbuckle my belt and pull my hard cock out. Precum leaks from the tip. She places her thumb on it and rubs in circles, spreading the sticky fluid around the engorged head. My body burns with desire, and a drop falls onto her abdomen. She runs her finger through it, lifting it to her lips and sucking. My dick twitches in anticipation of plunging into the warmth of her wet pussy. She grabs my hips and I lean forward. My cock is inches from her mouth, and she sticks her tongue out to lick at the tip, flicking it back and forth while she stares at me before she grabs hold of my ass, digging her fingers into my cheeks, making me jut forward from the pain. Mari uses this opportunity to fully take my dick into her mouth, and I almost come on the spot. I grab her hair and thrust in, hitting the back of her throat. I pull back when she gags, and she sucks hard on the tip, swirling her tongue under the shaft. My balls ache for release. I pull her mouth away from my cock with a *pop*, and a trail of her saliva falls across her chin. I bend down, kissing her with everything I have. Her arousal wafts through the air, making my erection painful, so I push her legs open.

I rip her lace panties off her body, bringing them to my nose and breathing in her scent. God, she smells so good. I spread her legs and lick through her folds. Lifting her ass with my hands, I present her pussy like a gift for the taking. I fuck her with my tongue just like I will with my cock until she screams, calling out my name as she rides my face.

Pulling away from her quivering cunt, I grab a condom out of my pocket before pushing my pants down the rest of the way as I rub my sheathed cock through her folds, adding lubrication to my shaft. She flips around onto her knees, picking her ass up in the air. My hand comes down hard on her ass before kneading it as I begin to push the head of my cock into her wet pussy. She gasps and leans back into me. "You're such a greedy girl for my dick, aren't you, baby?"

"Yes," she moans. "Fuck me, Chev." I hold her hips up and give her what she asks for, setting a punishing rhythm. My hips hit her ass, and my balls smack against her, shoving her forward. Her head falls forward on the pillows, and her hands clutch the sheets.

"God, Mari, you take my cock so well. I can feel your hot cunt gripping my dick, baby." She moans, and I know that she is close to coming again. This time, I want to be closer to her, so I flip us so she straddles me. Her eyes are wild with lust as she hovers over me. "Ride me, baby. Own me." She lines herself up with my cock and sinks to the hilt. We both moan in unison at the deep sensation. She does what I say and takes what she needs. I thrust my hips upward as she bounces up and down on my cock. I grasp her hips, pushing her further until her walls squeeze my cock, and I come as she milks me dry.

I hold her there until we are satiated, and she leans forward, falling on my chest. I hold the condom as she lifts herself off and collapses onto the bed beside me. I dispose of it in the bathroom and crawl back into bed with her. I pull her close to me and kiss the side of her face. I stare at her like a lovesick fool. Her breathing is even as she quickly falls asleep, and I decide that I have never been so grateful for a spilled iced matcha latte.

CHAPTER
TWENTY-EIGHT

MARI

Chev leans over and places a light kiss on my cheek before getting up, the bed dipping under his weight. The sheets already lack warmth from the loss of his body heat. I can hear him zipping and buckling up his pants. His boots sound on the floor as the bed dips on my side. I open one eye, and his smile lights up the whole room. "Hey, baby." He reaches up and strokes my cheek. "I have to help my mom this morning at the cafe, but I'll meet you at the commons for lunch, and then we can walk to class together?"

I hold the sheets to my body, and he meets me halfway to kiss me. I plop back onto the pillow. "Okay, I'll see you then.

I'll walk you out."

He holds his hand out for me to stop. "Sleep a little longer, Mari. I'll let myself out."

CHAPTER
TWENTY-NINE

MARI

After my first class that morning, I walk outside with a bit of pep in my step. I feel deliciously sore between my legs. I might be more tired if I wasn't on cloud nine, but nothing could sour my mood.

I walk into the bathroom to use the facilities. A toilet flushes behind me, and someone walks to the sink. Our hands simultaneously reach out to grab the soap. "Sorry," I say, glancing over at the girl as her eyes meet mine in the mirror. I quickly duck my head down, but not fast enough because I see her turn toward me and tilt her head as if trying to place where she's seen me.

"Do I know you?" she asks. "I've seen you before at Nate's house, right?" She's still trying to piece the puzzle together.

I shrug noncommittally. "Maybe?" I grab a paper towel and dry my hands off. I really don't want to rehash this. It's old news.

"Oh!" she exclaims, fingers snapping. "You're the flower delivery driver, right?"

I stare at her, wanting to tell her the truth. "Not exactly—"

"You know," she continues, "you left the other arrangement on the steps. The other girl never got her flowers." Her lips purse.

Instead of cowering, I decide on honesty. "Oh, I got them all right."

Her gaze snaps to mine, and her eyes narrow. "What do you mean?"

I sigh. "Look, those flowers were mine. Nate sent us both flowers, and they mixed the cards up with the arrangement. I went to his house to confront him on who 'Maxi' was, and then I met you."

"He's cheating on me?" Her hand covers her mouth, poorly masking her shock.

I shrug. "Well, technically, Nate was cheating on *me* because we had been together over that past year, but I'm not sure that we were the only ones." The realization sets in, and instead of waiting around for the worst-case scenario here, I walk off.

"Mari? Is that your name?" I turn around to look at her, and I see sadness in her eyes. "You're too good for him, Mari. Thank you for telling me. And you know what?" I wait because those are not the words I expected her to say after I hit her with the truth. "I'm too good for him, too." She walks past me and out the door, leaving me open-mouthed. Her words take me aback, but I admire her strength to realize her worth. I stifle a laugh, wishing I could see Nate's face when she confronts him.

I walk toward the commons and find Chev sitting at a table under our favorite tree, along with Lilith, Rory, and some of our other friends. Chev is talking to Mason when he sees me approach, and he stands, taking my book bag from my shoulder. I swing my legs around and sit beside him as my friends greet me warmly.

"Where were you, baby? I was going to look for you to see if you were okay."

I smile at his kind words and then see Maxi storming off in the distance. Chev follows my line of sight. Nate trails behind her, calling her name, but she doesn't acknowledge him. Maxi sees me and waves, smiling at us as she enters a building, leaving a very distraught Nate outside.

Lilith hits me on the shoulder. "Did you see that? What was that about, Mari?" I suppress a laugh.

"That, my friend, was karma…and it's a bitch." We all laugh together. My heart is full. It's a wonder what a couple of days can do to change someone's outlook on life. And to think it all started with a heart-shaped box, some heart-shaped candies, and my heart that will forever be whole because I know that I am loved.

EPILOGUE

FIVE YEARS LATER

CHEV

"Do you think she'll like it, Lil?" I stand there with my hands in my pockets as Lil and Rory invade my personal space. I watch them as they hold the ring with fascination and, dare I say, awe. Of course, when I was looking for rings I asked her best friend and her moms for help. They told me about the round-cut diamonds she loves, but I thought a little out of the box, or should I say, *heart-shaped box* on this one.

They were so overjoyed that they hugged and kissed my face repeatedly while I batted them away. Rory nods while Lil smiles. "You did good, Chevy." I give it another glance, seeing the sparkles radiate and echo off in prisms of light surrounding the cafe walls.

Mari will be here to meet me in a few minutes for dinner. In true Mari fashion, she's late. I start to pace, repeating what I want to say. Finally, she walks in through the door. The wind chimes echo her arrival, and my heart stops as I'm rendered speechless. She's breathtaking.

She looks like she's mine.

MARI

Chev tracks my movements. I walk in wearing a fitted red sleeveless dress that flares at the waist with a tiny black patent belt that accentuates my figure. I bought this dress in a little boutique here in town. I knew I had to have it for tonight when I saw it in the window. I've purchased a pair of matching black peep toe pumps. I completed the outfit with the dainty firefly pendant that houses a small diamond in the middle. Chev gave me on our one-year anniversary together. I rarely take it off. My long, dark hair flows down my back in waves. Nothing else matters. Nothing else exists as I walk to meet him, although a bit fashionably late, but from what I can see from the heat in his eyes, I know he doesn't mind the extra time I took to get ready for him.

I lift my manicured fingers, running over the fabric of his sports coat. "You look handsome tonight. Did you get dressed here?" He looks over to the spot where I usually sit, and I track his movements. That's when I notice Lil and Rory finishing their beverages in the corner. My mouth twitches, tilting my head in their direction.

"Wow. That was hot," I hear Rory tell Lil, and my cheeks redden. I look down, embarrassed, but Chev lifts my chin with his finger, forcing my face upward. He knows that I only have eyes for him.

A silent conversation passes between us. *I know, baby. I only have eyes for you, too.* He continues to hold me captive with his heated stare.

Lil and Rory stand, gathering up their items. "I'll be right back," Chev says and then mutters something about "setting the plan into motion." A minute or two passes before he calls for me from the back of the cafe.

"Mari! Can you come back here, please?" My heels click across the floor as I reach him.

I look at him quizzically, standing there facing me. "What did you need?" I ask. His throat bobs, and then the sound of the door closes behind me with a click. I turn toward the door and walk over, trying to open the handle, but it's locked. I spin back around, eyes wide.

"Chev? What is going on?" He walks up to me slowly.

"There are three things I want to say to you." He reaches into his jacket pocket and pulls out a box of candied hearts.

My eyebrows waggle upward. "My favorite chalky candy, Chev. You really shouldn't have." And then it hits me. "This all seems too familiar."

I laugh, shaking my head. It's been our running joke since we were stuck in the pharmacy storeroom. It doesn't go unnoticed as he looks fondly at me.

He nods. His eyes crease in contemplation before he opens the box. "Hold out your hand." I do as he says, extending my hand in front of me. A smile pulls at my lips at his orders. He takes a heart out and places it in my palm. He doesn't bother looking at it. This was clearly planned.

My fingers shake as I pick up the candy heart and read it aloud. "Be mine." My eyes soften. Before I can even think, I answer, "I already am."

"And I'm yours." He pulls the next candy out of the package slowly before placing it into my palm, almost like he is anticipating the words. He says, "Say yes," and drops to one knee.

I gasp. "C-Chev."

He pulls out a heart-shaped diamond ring from the box. He clears his throat. "This ring symbolizes my eternal love for you, Mari. I think we were always going to get to this point once I saw you on the dance floor that day. This symbolizes our true love and my promise to love you until our dying day."

Tears form in my eyes. "Yes, absolutely, yes. One hundred matcha lattes and nasty-tasting, heart-shaped candies, yes." My hands go to my mouth as a sob escapes.

He stands up and places the ring on my shaking finger. He removes the last heart-shaped candy from the box. "This one says: kiss me." I drop the candy onto the floor and jump into his arms, wrapping mine around his neck. His mouth meets mine in a hungry kiss. We kiss until I'm panting, reaching for his zipper and pulling it down. He stops me, also breathless, and I pull back, seeing his lips are swollen and his eyes are hooded. I stare at him, wondering how I became this lucky and what I did to deserve him.

"Why do you look at me like that?" His eyes sparkle with mischief.

I smile, meeting his lips. "How do I look at you?"

He mouths the words into them. "Like I love you?" He kisses me, and I can feel his lips curve upward. I pull back to gaze at him. "Like I've been sick until you?" He continues with his declarations.

My eyebrows rise in question. "Lovesick?"

He nods. "I want to be lovesick, Mari, only to find that you are my cure." He brings his lips back down to mine, and I reach into his pants and wrap my hand around his thick cock.

There's a knock on the door, and the handle turns. I remove my hand from his pants. "Are you guys done in here? I didn't hear any noises, so..." Lil trails off. She sees the ring on my finger, and she yells, "She said yes!" There's an eruption of cheers from the cafe. Chev turns around, coughing, trying to pull up his zipper, and Lil makes an O-shape with her mouth. Her lips quirk up in a silent laugh as she walks away.

"Was there ever any doubt?"

"I really hoped not," Chev says as he leads me out of the storage room. Hand in hand, we walk out and see the small gathering of our friends and family ready to celebrate with us.

And I now think Valentine's Day is my favorite day of the year. Not because of the candy or flowers, but because of the meaning of love. What it truly means to be loved. As I look out over my family, friends, and now my future husband, I realize what love really is. It's not in the gifts on one special day, but in your deep connection with someone who accepts you for who you are. I've also found what I wanted more than anything—to truly be seen.

THE END

Did you enjoy reading *Heart-Shaped Box?* If so, please take a
second to leave a review on one or all of your choices below.
Reviews help to make me a better writer, and I appreciate
your words and constructive criticism!
Love you all,

L. Renée Richard

Amazon:
https://a.co/d/1AiS7Nb

Goodreads:
https://www.goodreads.com/user/show/43246025-l-renee-
richard

BookBub:
https://www.bookbub.com/authors/l-renee-richard

OTHER BOOKS BY L. RENÉE RICHARD

Waves of You

Torn between two turbulent loves, she's engulfed by the waves of fate.

Paperback, E-book, and free on KU

https://a.co/d/e2WJp5o

Black Wave: A Forged Hearts Novel

She lost everything to him. Now, the only thing she has left is vengeance.

Paperback, E-book, and free on KU

Book 1 of the Forged Hearts Series

https://a.co/d/fu05pGA

Twisted Tides

He stole their past. They'll reclaim their future.

Paperback and e-books are free on KU.

Book 2 of the Forged Hearts Series

https://a.co/d/e8zfWBL

ABOUT THE AUTHOR

L. Renee Richard is a Hispanic author who lives in rural New England with her family. She's a born and raised South Texan girl who implements BIPOC characters into her books, imbued with her cherished Hispanic culture. She is an avid reader, complete with her never-ending TBR, and a romantic at heart who appreciates strong female main characters and good book boyfriends in the books she reads or writes. She loves summers in New England, sitting on the beach with a book, driving with the windows down through rural roads on cool autumn nights, and iced matcha lattes. Her books promise angsty romance where the journey to a happily ever after isn't always easy, but it's worth the trip.